Y0-BYO-849

Transgressions

ALSO BY SALLIE BINGHAM

After Such Knowledge
The Way It Is Now
The Touching Hand and Six Short Stories
Passion and Prejudice: A Family Memoir
Small Victories
Matron of Honor
Straight Man
Upstate

Transgressions

STORIES Sallie Bingham

Sarabande Books
LOUISVILLE, KENTUCKY

Copyright © 2002 by Sallie Bingham.

All rights reserved

No part of this book may be reproduced without written permission
of the publisher. Please direct inquiries to:

Managing Editor
Sarabande Books, Inc.
2234 Dundee Road, Suite 200
Louisville, KY 40205

LIBRARY OF CONGRESS CATALOGING-IN-PUBLICATION DATA

Bingham, Sallie.
Transgressions : stories / by Sallie Bingham.– 1st ed.
p.   cm.
ISBN 1-889330-77-9 (cloth : acid-free paper) – ISBN 1-889330-92-2
(pbk. : acid-free paper) 1. Feminist fiction, American. 2. Women –
Fiction. I. Title.
PS3552.I5 T73 2002
813'.54–dc21   2002001259

Cover image: *Exchange*, oil on canvas, 40" x 72", by Ron Richmond
Provided courtesy of the artist

Cover and text design by Charles Casey Martin

Manufactured in the United States of America
This book is printed on acid-free paper

Sarabande Books is a nonprofit literary organization.

Publication of this book was funded in part by a grant from the
Kentucky Arts Council, a state agency of the Education, Arts, and
Humanities Cabinet.

FIRST EDITION

For Francis

Table of Contents

Apricots / 1

Benjamin / 13

A Remarkably Pretty Girl / 31

The One True Place / 41

The Big Bed / 57

Stanley / 73

The Pump / 85

Rat / 101

The Hunt / 117

Loving / 145

The Splinter / 161

"Though I speak with the tongues of men and of angels, and have not charity, I am becoming as sounding brass, or a tinkling cymbal."

I Corinthians 13

Acknowledgments

The author would like to thank
the editors of the following magazines,
in which these stories appeared
in somewhat different form:

Confrontation
"Benjamin"
The Georgetown Review
"Stanley"
The Greensboro Review
"The Big Bed"

Transgressions

Apricots

That June Caroline's apricot tree finally bore fruit. In the six years she'd lived in the house behind the tree, late frost had nipped its buds in April and only a few dwarfed apricots had hung on the branches. Neighbors said the apricot trees were not native to northern New Mexico but were brought as seedlings in the saddlebags of the Spanish conquest; over the centuries they had not adapted to the harsh climate, but neither had they died. All along Caroline's dirt road, the tall conical shapes stood out in winter and, in a rare spring, were thickly hung with white blossoms and bees.

Living alone after a lifetime of living with other people granted Caroline time and leisure that had mystified and depressed her at first—where were the faces that used to surround her kitchen table, where were the feet that had pounded on her stairs?—but that lately had seemed the only real luxury life had ever, or could ever offer: to lie in bed late, dozing until the sun slid into her window and across her bed, a blade of hot brass; to eat alone off a tray in this or that corner of the house or garden; to fall asleep, sometimes, on the porch, while a summer storm rattled overhead, then gave way to stars and the pondering moon. To Caroline at sixty-three it seemed all the nature that surrounded her sustained her—the moon in its silver cycles, the pink-red geraniums and long flowing native grasses in her garden, and now the apricot tree itself with its bridal finery that didn't droop and was replaced, overnight, it seemed, with an astonishing crop. All pondered, all watched from within their private and separate existences.

At first she picked all the apricots she could and filled bowls and baskets where the fruit fermented, giving off a sweet perfume that reminded her of the candy shops of her childhood. She hated to throw out all that luxury, that unprecedented generosity, but at first she could not think of an alternative. For a few days she let the fruit drop from the tree and ground it under the tires of her car every time she went in and out; that was an unacceptable waste. Finally she remembered another scene from her childhood, of women sweating, chatting, bending over pots on a stove, and she decided to do some canning.

For a city woman, once a New York City woman, at that, the idea of spending a day in a hot steamy kitchen was, at first, unthinkable, but she remembered all the friends who would prize squat jars of apricot jam, and how a few of those jars would blaze on her pantry shelf in the depths of winter. And so she went out and bought four large, light aluminum pots, bigger than any pots she had ever owned, and after some searching, discovered that the cardboard trays of quilted jam glasses she remembered were still available, along with the white oblongs of paraffin needed to seal the tops.

But the task was daunting and Caroline soon realized she would have to have help. The steps in her mother's cookbook were complicated, especially the dry insistence on blanching the fruit to remove the skins, then processing them to prevent darkening. (Caroline was not sure why the fruit should not darken since she did not remember anyone in the old days caring what color it was.)

She pondered the situation for several days, meanwhile accumulating more bowls and baskets of apricots, which she kept in her refrigerator. Going out early in the morning to pick up what had fallen during the night, she would stop for a moment and stand with her hands on her hips, looking at the huge, glittering thunderheads already piling up in the west. Then she would bend to the task, feeling for a moment not like a sophisticated older woman released at last from unproductive demands but like a nymph loose in some glade in Arcady. Her yard and drive were not equal to that picture but she herself was, she believed, with her ocher-colored hair and long limbs and alert, unlined face.

Then it occurred to her that one of the young men in the class she taught at the local college might be willing to help. The class had not been a particular success, from Caroline's point of view; the students were listless and her attempt to interest them in the poetry of the Modernists largely failed. But there was one among them who seemed to have a spark of willingness; sometimes she caught young Charles Cooper's eyes fixed upon her as she lectured.

The semester ended shortly, and when she met with her students to hand them their graded finals and speak—she hoped—a few words of wisdom about the importance of E. E. Cummings and H.D., Caroline had made up her mind. As the little group gathered itself to leave, she signaled to Charles who, as usual, was watching. He came to her desk promptly.

"I have a job I want to do—a domestic job," she added, realizing he would think it was something involving reading or writing. "My apricot tree is covered with fruit and I want to put up some jam."

He looked at her alertly. He was a slight, sharp-faced young man with brownish hair brushed straight back and oddly freckled green eyes. His hands and feet, she had already noticed, were small, but his legs were long and his arms, below the short sleeves of his shirt, were tanned and supple.

"Okay," he said, a little too quickly, she thought.

"Of course I'm planning to pay."

"That won't be necessary," he said, turning away. She had to call him back to explain that she needed a morning later that week, and to give him her address; as he listened, she felt sheepish. It was an unfamiliar sensation, not entirely unpleasant.

The day arrived with thunderheads, brilliant sun, and heat. Caroline got up early to gather the last windfalls; she now had seven containers of apricots, and her small kitchen soon filled with their sweet, narcotic perfume. She took a shower and dressed, then found herself, unaccountably, taking off her shorts and shirt and putting on a dress; she realized that if she had possessed such a thing as a housedress and apron, she would have put them on, not as a disguise (as she would have thought, even the day before) but as a proclamation of some kind. What the words in the proclamation were she did not know.

She filled the largest kettle and set it on the stove to boil water for the jam jars. As she took the jars off their tray, she felt their quilted sides and looked with admiration at the anonymous fruits that decorated their lids. The jars, which normally she would hardly have noticed, seemed like master-pieces of artistry to her; who could have devised the quilted pattern of the glass, or left such a cunning space on one side for a label?

Presently she heard a light knock, and went to let in Charles. She was struck by the fact that he came to the front door, obscured by walls and trees, rather than to the more accessible kitchen door. "That apricot tree is covered," he said by way of greeting, standing in front of her, poised as though to turn in any direction, or to leave.

"I've picked about all we can manage today," she said, gesturing toward the bowls. Charles put out his hand and picked up an apricot, which he slipped, whole, into his mouth. Smiling, he said, "That's the first one of those I've ever eaten. It's good!"

"Are you from around here?" It was, she realized, the first personal question she had ever asked him.

He shook his head. "Maine."

They set to the task at once; later, Caroline wondered if she should have offered him something, first—coffee, or a glass of water. She knew young men usually jumped out of bed and ran out with no breakfast to whatever the day offered; she had raised three sons herself, and remembered their mixture of lassitude and spontaneity, which had so baffled her at the time. Charles, she assumed, was hungry; but when, later on, she asked him, he said he had already cooked and eaten a perfectly adequate breakfast.

They quickly sorted out the tasks, working side by side at the counter as smoothly, Caroline thought, as though they had been working together for years. She undertook the blanching (the jars were sterilized by now and laid out to cool on a linen towel), dropping the apricots by handfuls into boiling water, then quickly lifting them out. Drained, the apricots went to Charles, who shucked off their skins; the pile of darkening yellow-and-orange skins grew by his elbow as the kitchen filled with the dense sweetness of the hot fruit.

"Do you really think darkening is a problem?" Caroline asked him as she studied the dogeared cookbook, its cover a map of kitchen stains.

"They look better light," he said with authority.

He began dropping the peeled apricots into a solution of salt, vinegar, and water, and the piercing smell of the vinegar was added to the apricots' sweetness.

"Oh dear, I'm afraid I should have reheated them first," Carolyn said after she had read the recipe again, but Charles reassured her that the fruit was still hot from the blanching process.

Caroline stopped for a moment to watch him. His small, tanned hands moved regularly across the counter as he shucked the apricots and dropped them into the solution; he was frowning with concentration, lost in the task, she thought, until he asked, gruffly, "What are you looking at?"

"You. I never thought I'd see any of you young men in my kitchen."

"Why not?"

"I only know you in terms of my class," she said.

"I used to help my mother a lot," he explained, as though this was not the most interesting answer to the question she implied.

"I expect she's about my age," Caroline said, returning to her blanching.

"I don't know. How old are you?"

"Sixty-three," she said proudly. She had never stooped to lying about her age.

"Why did you never bother to get to know any of us?" he asked abruptly.

Caroline was startled. It had not occurred to her that anything she had done, or not done, in the class had had a consequence.

"You never even learned all our names," Charles went on. "Last week you called Todd Franklin Frank."

"I always mix up those names that could be first or last," she equivocated. Really he had embarrassed her and she wished suddenly that he would go.

"That's not the reason you called him Frank," Charles said. "You just didn't care enough to figure us out."

Caroline stopped what she was doing and leaned on her hands. Looking down, she saw the age spots rise from her skin

like the spots on the back of a toad; she saw the little sacks of
skin around her knuckles and wondered when they had come
there. "I did the best I could," she said and knew, instantly, that
it was not true.

"Taste one of these," Charles said, and he handed her a
peeled apricot.

Without its fuzzy skin, the apricot looked small and
vulnerable, like a naked part of a person that would ordinarily
be hidden. Caroline slipped it into her mouth and brought her
teeth down lightly; the soft meaty flesh of the apricot fell away
onto her tongue. It was deliciously sweet, and hot.

"You have one, too."

Charles slid an apricot into his mouth and smiled at her. "I
forgive you," he said.

Instantly she was angry. "For what?"

"Not caring."

"Do all your other teachers care?" she asked.

"Some do, some don't. But I always find a way to tell the
ones who don't. For their own good," he added mischievously.
"I could tell you were disappointed in the class, you might
want to know why it didn't work."

"I thought it was the reading list," she said.

"There's nothing wrong with those writers." To prove his
point, he quoted one of them, but Caroline could not identify
the line.

"I'm sorry," she said.

Charles seemed satisfied. "Let's save some of these last ones to eat later."

She agreed, and they sorted out several handfuls of the cooked apricots and put them on a china plate. The china plate was decorated with a stylized bird and a farmer, in blue on yellow, and Caroline remembered with a shock (she had not thought about this in years) that as a child she had often eaten her breakfast off this plate.

At last they put twelve filled jars to sterilize in the popping, boiling kettle. The kitchen windows were blind with steam and the heat was overpowering. Caroline suggested taking the saved apricots outside.

She and Charles sat on the doorstep and ate them. One by one, they fed them into their mouths. At some point, without a word, Charles pushed an apricot into her mouth, and Caroline laughed with surprise. "Why did you do that?"

"Just to see."

She spit the dark, smooth oval seed into her hand and studied it.

They finished the apricots—Caroline anticipated an upset stomach, she had eaten so many—and went back into the kitchen. Charles fished the hot jars out of the sterilizer and pulled up the rack, and Caroline inserted the remaining jars.

As Charles lowered them into the boiling water, a plume of steam obscured his face. Then he slapped on the lid.

"So masterful," Caroline said, laughing. In the back of her mind a sort of clock was ticking, telling off the details of the plans she had made for the afternoon: a visit to the post office to mail her sister's birthday present, some cleaning to pick up. The clock ticked and ticked but it seemed to have removed itself to some other part of the house.

Charles laid his hand over her hand on the counter. "I think you're very attractive," he said.

"Oh, honestly. I'm old enough to be–"

"Why do you keep harping on age?"

"Because it's the truth. Or part of it," she added uneasily.

His hand slid up her arm to her shoulder, bare under the strap of her dress. "You have an amazing body."

She was speechless. The feel of his palm on her bare shoulder reminded her of the texture of her own skin, which she treated now like a commodity, washing and drying it mechanically. She tried to remember other touches, other times, but it seemed that the years between had blotted out the memory. She flushed and breathed deeply, trying to regain her balance. "What are you doing, Charles?" she asked.

His hand moved from her shoulder to her waist as he turned her. "Kissing you," he said, and did.

Later Caroline remembered the flesh of the apricots, their slight graininess, the moisture that was not dripping like the sweetness of peaches but absorbed, contained. She remembered the wooly feel of the apricots' skins, and the smooth, shining brown pits. She even remembered the seam that ran up one side of each pit, and she also remembered the way the thick sweet smell of the cooking apricots had been cut by the tang of vinegar. And she longed to know what the apricots had meant, and continued to mean, even as she realized with dismay that her life was falling apart; the ticking of the clock had stopped and might never start again. With equal dismay and exhilaration, she remembered a line from one of the poets she had tried so unsuccessfully to teach her class that spring:

> "that is why I am afraid;
> I look at you,
> I think of your song,
> I see the long trail of your coming."

That was said by an old poet of a young poet. Could it not also be said by an old woman of a young man?

Benjamin

On his flight to the West Coast, lunch has just been served (Benjamin, who is ninety, has been quick to ask for the last slice of pizza, leaving the more abundant grizzled chicken salad to his seatmate), and the intercom is announcing that all uneaten food items should be set aside for the homeless.

The intercom adds, with unction, that this airline has instituted a new program, to cut down on waste and serve the less fortunate; with the side of his fork, Benjamin mashes his uneaten triangle of dark-berried pie.

"Please don't give this to the homeless," he says as he hands his tray to the flight attendant, whom in his mind he still calls a stewardess.

She glances at the mashed pie, makes a smile. "Oh, Mr. Price! I was just reading about your mural in that homeless center—where is it?"

"Detroit." He sets his lips. Now his seatmate is listening. "They have a big wall there. I had something I wanted to paint on a big wall." He does not treat the two women to a description of the squabble that followed when the center people refused to string a rope in front of his mural. Benjamin can imagine the effect of dispossessed shoulders and hands on his chalky rendition of the famous naked picnic, featuring local magnates—which had caused less stir than he had anticipated.

The flight attendant, clucking her refusal to be dismayed, moves on; she knows her celebrities, their disposition to the difficult. Nothing Benjamin can say or do, short of murder, will dim the glow she takes away from the encounter.

Benjamin's seatmate, a blond woman wearing snail-shaped gold earrings (she laid aside a roll, he's noticed, for the dispensation) glances at him uneasily.

"I don't believe in the poor," he says in his high, ratcheting voice. "I've always been poor—until very recently; it's a decent, serviceable condition. 'The poor are always with you,'" he quotes, betting she won't get it. "Why should we work against the Gospels?"

The woman looks at him sheepishly, as though she has a moral responsibility to upbraid him but can't think of the necessary words. Possibly she is sheepish because she doesn't recognize him. "My mother used to volunteer in a shelter," she offers.

"Either she was a fool or she had nothing better to do or both."

She turns the fixed jaw of pained dismay and looks determinedly at her magazine.

Missing her response, Benjamin remembers the years when Ida sat beside him and fended off the not-always unwelcome advances of strangers. Sometimes he'd take an aisle seat, leaving Ida the window, in order to engage in unauthorized talk with the person across the way. Especially if it was a woman. Ida was robust and charmless, a personal assistant addicted to the personal (she cleaned his ears with Q-tips, bought his boxer shorts in packages of six), who never aspired to the status such intimacy presumably confers. Which was why he'd kept her for eleven years until, tearful over her wasted youth, she insisted on departing; at that point Benjamin decided to make do with a grad student two afternoons a week.

In spite of all the commissions, his mail is decreasing, his phone rings less, and he is beginning to suspect his spectacular age is losing its ability to draw attention to his work. But he has all the mechanisms of avoidance in place: the answering machine, the fax, the computer with its self-satisfied digestion of unwanted data. He plans never to figure that one out.

Now the intercom announces that they are about to land

in Los Angeles. His seatmate takes two Styrofoam cups from her enormous bag and sticks the open ends over her ears. All the way down to the ground, Benjamin watches as she shrinks into herself, closing her eyes and hunkering over her knees.

"What's with the cups?" he asks when they're taxiing and she's taken them down.

"I have earaches," she tells him with a dismissive shrug. "Terrible earaches! This way I create a vacuum."

Now the jetway is rolling out like a serpent bound to devour its prey and Benjamin feels the shortness of time.

"But what about the air already inside the cups?" he asks. When she looks startled, he explains, "You can't suck the air out that's already in there, so how can you create a vacuum?"

She continues to look distressed, so Benjamin whips out his salvaged paper napkin and begins to draw one of her ears, in ink. The ear is clutching its earring. He signs the drawing, then passes it to her; she takes it gingerly, between two fingers, as though it might be infected. "Send that to Sotheby's if you're ever short of money."

"I thought you were somebody," she says, folding the drawing carefully and stowing it in a zippered compartment of her bag.

Then Benjamin follows her out of the plane, noting with pleasure that her butt is more shapely than her face has led him to expect.

She disappears into the crowd as the usual contingent comes forward to meet him. Benjamin leans away from the introductions, trying not to hear. Lately he's let the word go round that he's going deaf, yet refuses to wear one of those navel-colored hearing aids. In fact his hearing, like his eyesight, is uncomfortably keen.

They herd him through collecting his baggage and into a car.

He notices that the girl driving has a pretty neck, tendriled with dark hair. From the backseat (he has insisted on sitting there, claiming it makes him feel safer), he traces each tendril with his forefinger.

The girl reaches up as though to slap a fly; her boss, the museum director, shakes his head and she drops her hand. Benjamin can tell from the set of her shoulders that she is expecting the attention to go on—they'll be saying he's senile, next, giving him still more room to play—but he has become absorbed in watching the light change in the oily water running down the gutters. Apparently it has just stopped raining.

He finds the obscure tablet that opens the window and breathes the moist, fetid air. "I love the sheer unhealthiness of cities," he says, and has to put up with the museum director's comfortable chuckle.

Years ago, in his early eighties, with his first fame, his first money, Benjamin tried to explain that what he said, no matter how outrageous, was not said for effect. It made no difference how he scowled, or growled. He has become an old, harmless painter of great and safe distinction, a kind of greeting card, he thinks, offered to artists on the threshold of age. "Hold on a while longer and this is what you'll get."

The museum director, an affable smiling blond man, whom Benjamin would have guessed scarcely out of his twenties if his title did not confer more age, lets him out at an old downtown hotel, a rookery refurbished now that the neighborhood is becoming prosperous. "For the atmosphere," the young man explains, hoisting Benjamin's suitcase out of the trunk. "All the old Hollywood stars used to stay here." He sees Benjamin through the signing-in process and the bestowal of the card that passes for a room key while the girl waits in the car.

"I like that young girl of yours," Benjamin says as the director is ushering him into a gilded elevator.

"She's not mine," the man says, handing him his suitcase.

"Then the museum's. I'm hoping she'll be at dinner tonight."

"The whole staff will," the young man says without emphasis. They are back on the flat ground of arrangements where, Benjamin thinks as the elevator glides up, no passion or appetite ever raises its head.

In his room, he lies down on a snake-colored bedspread and stares at the painting on the wall: a vast, naked-looking melon, poised like a threat over some harmless cherries. He remembers when he was grateful for such a sale, did not even wince when the hotel asked him to hang the piece, for free; remembers going into rooms like this, dank with emptiness, smelling in those days of the last inhabitant's cigarettes, scrabbling his hand along the wall for the light switch, blinking in the glare at the bald gray or green walls. Where to put the child of his invention, the hapless orphan of an eyeless world? He falls asleep studying the strange shine on the sides of the cherries. A sort of feverish, fruity glow.

Up in time to shave, again—he lets the fact that he still needs to shave twice a day provide the meaning he needs—shower, and dress for the performance. His evening clothes, folded haphazardly, are wrinkled, and he thinks briefly of muscling the ironing board out of the closet, then abandons the notion. He likes his fluted purple dress shirt and polka-dot bow tie, and spit-polishes his patent-leather pumps with the tassels. Of course no one wears such clothes anymore, even to honorary dinners. Then he goes down to the lobby.

His old life returns as he waits in an armchair placed at an angle to a distressed-looking potted palm. In his twenties, he was night clerk in a hotel such as this one was a few years ago: plunging down into flophousehood. He'd been glad for the job, and turned it into a playground for his drawings of the inhabitants, which he kept on a sketchpad on his knees.

Then one night a distraught-looking man signed in late,

and some instinct warned Benjamin of trouble; he went up to check and found smoke spiraling from under the door and the man half-conscious on his lit bed. It took a while for the local fire department to rouse its members. Meanwhile Benjamin doused the man and the bed with water from a paper cup, the only receptacle at hand. The man remained comatose, although not badly burned, and was hauled off to the local hospital; when Benjamin visited him there, a few days later, more out of curiosity—he had begun to draw him—than any regard for his welfare, the man told him with shame about the usual progression: a divorce, a job setback, the alienation of some minor children.

Well, it is always the same in the end, Benjamin thinks as his host comes through the entrance with a carnation in his buttonhole and another, the old painter knows, in the white box he is carrying; in the end heartbreak, even death, boils down to a few inevitable details: desertion, disappointment, all on the human scale.

He allows the young man to fasten the carnation in his buttonhole, noticing that his is red while the director's is white. "Red as the blood in my veins," he jokes as the young man holds open the door and scoops his hand under his elbow to help him into the car, then feels, unexpectedly, foolish: it is all too obvious. But the young man has scarcely heard and feels no need to reply. This time, he is driving.

In the vast hotel ballroom—another hotel; this time, one of
a noxious chain—Benjamin looks around for the girl but does
not see her at first. He pantomimes extreme deafness and
distraction, holding his hand to his ear as a bevy of museum
supporters is led forward and introduced.

They are all middle-aged women, handsomely dressed,
and he knows how vital their support is to the museum, and
how heavily their support depends on the success of events
like this one. He believes these women have forgotten what it
was like to ward off a man's advances, and he feels for them,
briefly, and wishes that aging flesh, no matter how well-
preserved, did not ignite his uncontrollable disgust. He is a
man of his times, after all.

Then he sees the girl in a becoming black cocktail dress,
seated at the other end of the table—she is minor personnel, after
all, and it would have taken a cosmopolitan imagination to place
her near him. He waves his napkin and smiles, striking his
dinner companion dumb; she has been carrying on about a trip
somewhere, the art she has seen and absorbed, Benjamin
imagines, as a great sea-going turtle absorbs the green contents
of a wave. She is handsome as a sea turtle, too, in her smart green
scaly dress, but he is beyond being polite and fixes his eyes,
instead, on the discreet hint of bare breast the girl is displaying
in her décolletage. She wears one of the official white carna-
tions, pinned where it will draw attention to her charms.

She's conscious, then, he thinks with pleasure, of what her femininity can do, or could do, given the proper stage, which she assuredly lacks, and he is off at once, seeing her in silk lounging pajamas on the veranda of some gracious Tuscan villa, or striding out into the foam on a Caribbean beach. In his earlier days, women went for that kind of exchange, knowing that the less than satisfactory lover was likely to be replaced with the more satisfactory at a plumy resort; accepting, he thinks, even now, after all the changes, that there was a fairness in spreading one's beautiful and accommodating legs in return for opportunities that were not wholly–never wholly–financial. But a young girl would be ashamed to consider that, now.

His companion has struck up her talk again–it appears that Rome, and Paris, too, are still to be got through–and he leans toward her with the transparent fatigue of the elderly. She sees this at once and pats his shoulder consolingly. They are both in the same shallow canoe, hurrying down a darkening river. But he will reach the end long before she.

He notices the big diamond on her finger, and interrupts her soliloquy to ask about its purchaser.

While she details the well-memorized glories of her marriage, ended by the husband's death long enough ago to allow for the powers of reinvention, Benjamin doesn't take his eyes off the young girl. The swine on either side have not even bothered to notice her, being taken up with more important if less comely partners. Benjamin swallows his nearly-raw steak, bit by bit, and imagines opportunities.

The after-dinner toasts pass rapidly and he is only required to nod and smile, not to respond—another advantage of his age. It is presumed that he is exhausted from the long flight and the change in time, which in fact he has scarcely noticed. He allows waves of congratulation to pass over him while he drinks his coffee, well-laced with sugar and heavy cream. He has scornfully turned down someone's kindly suggestion that he might prefer decaf.

Now he feels his heart pounding, as it will do in spite of all his efforts to avoid noticing it, at the end of the day, after a lot of food and drink. (The champagne is a good French vintage and he has not stopped at his usual two glasses, even rising to clink and say something foolish about the honor.) As he pushes his chair back from the table, he feels his heart leaping like a demon under his purple shirt and stops to steady the leap with his palm.

Immediately the young director has his hand under his elbow and is suggesting a swift trip back to the rookery, and rest.

Benjamin shakes him off and makes a beeline across the room to the girl, chatting colorlessly with another woman.

She feels his approach as one might feel, Benjamin thinks, the approach of a heat-sensitive missile, and turns, her hand already up, palm out. He takes that as the greeting it is not and places his own palm against hers. How warm her skin is, how limpid.

"Drive me back to that hellish place and I'll buy you a drink," he says, hearing the thickness he hasn't felt on his tongue.

She glances at her boss, across the room, who must be nodding approval, or even insistence, then makes her manners to the various functionaries and tells Benjamin she will meet him at the front door.

Still he is not sure of her—they are slippery, these girls—and while the director is helping him into his overcoat and outlining the next day's heavy schedule, Benjamin is thinking of various face-saving devices. But then she is there, outside, sitting a little bowed in what is apparently her own car, a tiny red coupe, so low Benjamin has to double himself to get in. Once seated he straightens and fastens the belt as though he is girding on a sword.

At the click, the girl begins to drive, her pretty profile pointed forward like the figurehead on a small, stately yacht.

"I like you," he says, at once—there is no time left, in the whole world, it has run out to the last few grains in the hourglass—and without anticipating her response, he reaches over and fondles her breast. "I was admiring you all through that ghastly dinner, in that low-cut dress."

She has her instructions, and although she is not responsive, she does not shrug his hand away. He wonders, suddenly, if she is ambitious. Her black dress might suggest as much.

Then he feels her nipple harden under his fingers–ambitious, for sure; she is not wearing a bra–and crows his delight.

Of course she can't help it, she is driving, and also under instruction of some kind. Still he lets his fingers nuzzle the stiffness, and feels, to his amazement, a corresponding liveliness in his crotch. This is so rare now as to provide another crow of delight.

He keeps his hand on her nipple as she turns and glides the car through the downtown streets. When she draws up in front of his hotel, she does not cut the motor but remains staring fixedly straight ahead. "Come upstairs with me," he says, adding, "I'm a harmless old man, there isn't much I can do."

"I doubt that," she says, still staring straight ahead.

"Well, there may be a little, with your help. Have pity on a fellow sufferer," he adds, kissing her cheek. Her skin has the texture and taste of a slightly green apricot; it will be a few years before she reaches her full bloom. At the thought of her perhaps near-virginhood, he is aware of resources at the bottom of his spine he thought long ago dried up. "It isn't so often these days I can get this, just from touching a pretty girl's breast," he says, loosening her right hand from the steering wheel and guiding it to his crotch.

To his amazement, to his eternal delight, she turns, smiling slightly, and says she will go upstairs with him.

Later, in the grim light from the bedside lamp—she has wanted the dark, but he needs to peruse her—he is unable to remain hard long enough to enter her and lies, finally, on her frail, subsiding body, sobbing. His tears fall into the hollow at the base of her neck.

"I'm a stupid old goat," he tells her later as she is dressing, and tries to think of a way to cheer her. "You'll have so many men in your life—so many accomplished, adoring lovers. You'll forget this unfortunate business right away."

"But you're a great artist," she says, pulling up her hideous panty hose. How they disfigure her hips and distort her ass as she turns around to step into her shoes.

He laughs then, at the thought that she has imagined a great artist as a great lover. "I expect you'll have another great artist," he reassures her, "one young enough to satisfy your expectations."

"You could have used your mouth," she says, with a glance.

He sees in her glance everything he has ever wanted. It is only an instant, and then she is gone, closing the door with a nurse's dispatch.

His sleep that night is both deep, and deeply disturbed. In the morning, in spite of a fierce headache, he goes out into the street to look for a fancy jeweler, but the neighborhood is only slowly emerging from decades of decay and the shop he finds specializes in pawn.

He goes in, but the grimy rhinestones and battered turquoise express a despair that sends him fleeing.

Then it is time for the luncheon, and the unveiling of his painting.

Somehow he makes it through the smoked salmon and capers, through the vichyssoise and crab cakes; he is waiting to see if the girl will reappear. But this is a select group of big donors, and she is not high enough on the totem pole to be included.

Then, staggering a little from the wine and the coffee, he is escorted into the throne room, as it were, of the museum: the glacial marble gallery where his painting is hanging, hidden under a piece of golden damask.

He manages not to hear a word that is spoken and to fend off the looks of concern that are beginning to wing his way; he knows he is very pale, and he wipes his forehead on his sleeve. His perspiration feels cold as it dries, a clamminess that alarms him. But he will make it through, somehow; the girl is standing at the edge of the group. He is able to notice her Chanel knockoff, her neat navy bow.

Then a heavy gold tassel is placed in his hand, and he knows he must pull. He doubts that he has the strength, but the gold curtain is flimsily attached and comes down with a single tug.

And there it is, the painting of his prime.

First, he is shocked by the display of mastery—the fire-works of the painting itself—as though (and this he would prefer not to believe) he has never until now believed in his ability. The painting dazzles him as, apparently, it dazzles the others; there is a moment of silence, and then a gasp. He feels his own breath filling out the gasp and says, under his breath, "How did I know that much about how to...?"

Someone asks, avidly, for the end of the sentence, but he is beyond finding it. The maze of the past is winding its web around him—the jeweled streets of his youth spun now to spidery gold.

He steps closer, peers. The others draw in. He realizes for the first time that he can't see as clearly as he supposed; the vermilions and greiges swim as the oily water in the gutters swam on the drive from the airport.

He takes another step and realizes his nose is only inches from the painting's surface.

Now someone is at his elbow, subtly resisting his forward lunge. But he shakes the fellow off—is it the blond young director?—and closes the gap.

His eyes float across the surface of the painting which he has not seen or thought much about in thirty years, and he relishes each detail, each successful brush stroke, as though a fundamental doubt about his life is being resolved.

But when he steps back, finally—and he senses a sort of relief blooming around him, knows his reputation as a wrecker has preceded him and at least one person has feared he will actually harm his own work—he sees the painting as a whole, and whispers, "She never wanted me to paint her."

Now the girl is nearby—he can smell her light lemony fragrance—and he turns blindly in her direction. "She told me if I painted her, it would be the end," he says. "I didn't care much—I wanted the painting. I wanted the painting a good deal more than I wanted her, even at the beginning," he admits, with a dry laugh. "I don't think she knew that."

"I expect she did," the girl says, cupping his elbow.

He would like to shake off her unneeded support but cannot summon the strength. His elbow squats like a toad in her warm palm. He continues to examine the portrait, noting the details of the gilded lace fichu—Madeleine had insisted, once she'd finally agreed to the sitting, on dressing herself as a turn-of-the-century Philadelphia heiress—the sparkler attached to the red velvet over her small breast. Seeing that, he shapes his crabbed hand to the memory of that breast, its responsive nipple. Even when she was sobbing, or excoriating him for some imagined or real misbehavior, he could rouse her nipple with a single touch. "I liked her breasts," he tells the girl—the other people seem to have drawn away, or else he is simply, now, freed of being aware of them. "Her breasts were the best things about her."

"Were they," the girls says.

"Her breasts, and her hair," Benjamin goes on, squinting through the reeling darkness at Madeleine's black, piled hair. A stray curl is arranged, carefully, over her temple. He can't see her face—that wistful smile; her features are, mercifully, blotted out by a flesh-colored cloud. "And she had nice skin. Dead and gone these many years.

"These are pearls that were her eyes," he says, looking at the dazzler that tops her puffed hair; a sumptuous diamond, as large as an egg yolk. "She was very proud of that diamond," he says. "Her second husband. I heard she kept it, after the divorce. She was between the marriages when I met her," he adds.

"What was her name?"

As he turns to answer her—proud that he remembers, proud, that he has known her name all his life—Benjamin feels something tear. It is as though the fabric that has bound him tightly for so many years has at last given way. He hears the rent, feels something entering.

"Madeleine," he says, hoarding his breath so that he can say more. For he knows what must come next: he must tell the girl how he looked for a jewel, for her. He must ask her name, so he can remember.

A Remarkably Pretty Girl

At first all Cory remembered was waking up in the painter's room, somewhere far downtown, on a gray winter morning. It was snowing, and the window opposite the bed, although blocked by a brick wall three feet away, was beginning to fill up.

The room was very cold. Sitting up, she snatched the old plaid blanket up to her shoulders. And now it all came back:

The room was empty. A broken-backed divan, a card table, and a rickety chair loomed in the uncomfortable light. Utterly cheerless, she thought, glancing at the menacing little stove, squatting like a beast in the corner, and the big tin tub with a board over the top. She had heard such arrangements in old lower East side walk-ups described as both colorful and temporary (nearly all her friends were artists), but she'd never actually seen such a place. Her pleasure in the exotic was dulled by her growing conviction that she had been abandoned.

She began to look around the room for her clothes and shoes, scattered across the bare floor. Her underpants were slung on a lamp shade, although she'd been too drunk to notice kicking them off. It was now only a small satisfaction to notice that they were nice black silk.

She began to calculate the steps it would take to cover the space between the relatively safe haven of the bed (after all, she'd actually slept there) and her underpants on the lamp shade. Then she saw her dress (what color had it been, she wondered now, and only knew it would have been very short), her good warm winter coat, and her boots. Her stockings and garter belt were not to be seen; she thought they might have slid into some corner—and remembered, even now, how she had posed and arched, reaching behind her back to unfasten the hooks on the embroidered silk belt.

Had he noticed? Had he stopped unbuckling his belt (or whatever it was he was doing) to admire her?

He was a painter, after all, and she was, as a hairdresser once told her, "a remarkable pretty girl." Everyone else in her life had seemed to take this for granted as a truth that did not need to be expressed, which made the hairdresser's comment (and he, too, had lost name, face, and all distinguishing characteristics, although she believed she'd gone to him for years) important. For this fact, if it was a fact, which had seemed obvious to everyone else, had never existed, for her.

Finally she pushed her feet out of the bed. The bare floor was as cold as a stone. There was a tall, angular iron radiator in the corner, she noticed, but it seemed dead.

She tiptoed across the floor to the black silk underpants.

As she was pulling them on, she saw that the room narrowed at the opposite corner into an ell that led to a small window. The painter was standing in the ell with his back to her.

He was naked, and the gray light lay along his shoulders and buttocks, which she remembered now as being narrow. She had not seen that much of him the night before, but an impression remained of strictness, tensile strength. His right hand was on his hip, his elbow cocked in an attitude that reminded Cory of her mother's infrequent lectures. His left hand, at chest height, was moving.

Cory stepped to one side. Now she could see the small canvas propped on an easel, set at an angle to the window. The painter's brush, moving across it, left splotches of aqua and salmon.

She stood in her underpants and stared. The coldness of the room seemed to abate until she was suspended in neutrality. She watched the muscles in his back move as his hand moved the brush. Once, he hunched his shoulder, as she remembered seeing a horse stir a muscle to dislodge a fly. Perhaps her gaze was the fly. However, he did not seem in any way aware of her.

Now the radiator coughed and began to tick. At the same time, the light outside the blocked window brightened. It had stopped snowing.

Still the painter's brush moved slowly across the small canvas.

"I paint," he'd told her at the party the evening before. She remembered her surprise that he had said, "I paint," and not, "I'm a painter"—in that room where everybody was something.

At last she turned to look for her stockings and garter belt. They had slithered under the broken-backed divan and lay there, curled. She straightened them out and hooked the belt around her waist, then drew the cold nylon up over her thighs. Snapping the four garters, she felt the mournfulness of her routine—dressing herself was stripped of all nuance. She might have been stuffing a pillow into a case while her two-year-old son clamored for attention. Once, she'd caught sight of herself in a mirror, holding a corner of a pillow between her teeth as she pulled on the case. Such fierceness in that grip, such determination!

She picked up her dress, discarded on the card table beside a plate of dried-up food, and dropped it over her head. A little confidence returned to her now that she was clothed; the dress was pretty, and she knew she looked nice in it. She remembered how eager he had been to undress her—clamped that memory between her teeth as she had clamped the pillow.

Sitting on the side of the bed, she pulled on her serviceable boots, stained with salt from the long winter.

Then she sat with her hands on her knees and looked at the tumbled pillows in their grimy cases and the gray, disordered sheets. She nearly wept when she saw the blue scallop along the edge of the top sheet; what was the purpose, what was the use of that? The blanket she'd huddled under looked, now, as though it had come out of a boy's sleep-away camp trunk, as though it might smell of wood fires and melted marshmallows. But she didn't dare to smell it; she only touched the rough, hairy fibers with one finger.

As a child, she'd loved her special blanket, stroking her nose with its satin binding until she fell asleep.

The radiator set up a chorus of clanks and hisses. Heat began to seep into the room.

Cory stood up. Her coat was on the foot of the bed, meshed with the coarse blanket. She pulled the coat on, feeling the chill of the satin lining. It had lain, a discarded skin, on their feet all night.

Her purse was on the rickety chair. She slung it over her shoulder.

Until then, she had not planned anything. Now she hesitated, watching the painter's bare shoulders move as he leaned toward his easel.

After a moment, she said, "Well, I'm going." The room did not seem ready to receive those words.

She regretted them immediately. All she wanted was to speak in the proper code, the code suitable to the situation.

He turned. His face looked unfamiliar. Perhaps, at the party, she had never really looked at him.

"I'll get you a taxi," he said, but he did not put down his brush.

"Never mind. I think I'll walk a little." That, she knew, was the proper code.

"It's a long way." She felt the brush of his soft, dark glance. His thighs, belly, and chest, even his drooping penis, looked as utilitarian now as her legs had looked when she shoved them into her stockings.

"Goodbye," Cory said, wishing there was something heroic about it.

"Goodbye. Thank you. That was fun." The last was said over his shoulder as he turned back to the easel.

Fun, she thought. It sounded like a visit to the state fair. But fun was the correct word. She would never question it. Instead, she felt a slight satisfaction that she had been able to ride him on her little tin Ferris wheel up to its peak and was now, quietly, carrying him down and away.

She let herself out the door and groped her way down two flights of stairs. At the bottom, the hall was already a marsh of melting snow. Someone had left a broken umbrella propped in the corner, and a pair of old boots. Under the slush, squares of yellow and black marble were set in a checkerboard pattern. Cory wondered, again, what was the use, what was the purpose?

She let herself out of the scabbed front door after a short, desperate struggle with complicated locks.

She did not know the neighborhood. Cramped row houses alternated with forbidding warehouses, their jawlike doors shut tight. The sidewalk was hard-packed, beginning to ice; a few people stumbled or marched along it.

At the corner, an old woman was struggling with an armload of grocery bags; she dropped one, and Cory stooped to pick it up. Peering into the woman's face, as round and ridged as a cabbage inside her kerchief, Cory felt, suddenly, lighter. They stood together, for an instant—two women bearing their burdens.

"Thank you," the old woman said, with a strange accent.

Cory stepped out to cross the street. There was no traffic except for a bus, lumbering a block ahead. The street sign was covered with snow, and she walked another block before she realized where she was.

Now she was clumping along over unshoveled sidewalks.

As always after a storm, the city had shut down. There would be no taxis for hours, there was no sign of another bus, and she did not know where to find a subway station. There was nothing for it but to walk home–about a hundred blocks, she calculated.

As she walked, her daily life began to enfold her. At noon, her son would be coming back from his weekend with his father. Probably he would be cranky and overtired, not particularly glad to see her; he would drop his suitcase at her feet and flee to the television. His father would stand for a moment in the doorway, rocking back and forth, as though he had something important to say, but usually it was only a detail of their complicated arrangements. Cory would smile and agree to any change or modification. None of it mattered, really. Everything that mattered had split when their marriage came apart, and the resulting debris had little significance. Simply, it had ended. Finally he would say good-bye, cordially, and she would turn away to see what was in the refrigerator for lunch.

At that thought–the carefully-wrapped leftovers in the refrigerator, showing their dim colors through the plastic– Cory stopped her plodding progress through the snow. She was standing in front of a little grocery, shut up tight, and she saw her reflection in the window, between stacked cans: a girl in a nice warm winter coat, the same coat she'd worn at college, sent on by her mother when Cory's marriage ended and money was in short supply. Her reflection, in spite of the coat, seemed less substantial than the pyramid of soup cans.

Cory turned away, pushing her hands into her pockets. She'd left her gloves, she realized, at the party, her nice leather gloves with fur linings.

Pushing her hands into her pockets reminded her of the way the painter had placed one hand on his hip and grabbed the brush with the other. That had happened before she woke up, in the darkness of the very early morning; by the time she saw him, he was already fixed, and she was fresh out of the swamp of his bed and wondering about her clothes.

She felt as she continued to walk the oncoming rush of the years. The wild tides of the sixties would pass, sweeping away jetsam—diaphragms, hand mirrors, bankbooks—and she would let her girlhood, at last, pass with them. There would be many more men, many more rooms, although none of them would be as austere as the painter's; instead, good libraries, views over Central Park. Eventually, there would even be more children—and more sheets, more cups and forks and pans. Eventually it would begin to seem unlikely that anyone, even a hairdresser, had ever called her a remarkably pretty girl. And then she would begin to live.

There would be passion along the way, she imagined: more black satin underpants, more crumpled sheets. Her passion would be for her men and for her babies; it would pass when the babies were out of diapers, and when their fathers began to doze after dinner. In its place, she would put her work–a worn briefcase stuffed full of appeals and protests; she would become quite good at fund-raising even as her own financial cares increased. After a while she would begin to describe the sixties as the decade when they all started doing things, all the people she knew burrowing into offices, storming out of marriages, carrying bagfuls of outdated party clothes to the Salvation Army.

But through it all–the blurring of chaotic events and the gradual clearing as she, growing old, gathered herself to endure the death of the one man she would love and the departure of her children–the painter's naked back as he stood at his easel that winter morning would float occasionally to the surface of her memory. She knew what his back meant, now; she understood, at last, his persistence in the face of cold and poverty and whatever it had seemed she had, briefly, promised. She would even feel, some mornings, the vibration in the soles of her feet that had raised him from the warm, tumbled bed.

Now, in the mornings, alone at last, she flexed her feet and spread her toes, waiting to feel the vibration that would spring her into her future, where there was only persistence, and dedication, and the way at last was clear.

The One True Place

The boy was given his first cherries that June—not the first cherries of his life; he'd been staining his mouth red since childhood from his grandmother's tree, in Taos—but the first cherries ever put into his hands.

He opened his hands when Tim, who also worked at the supermarket, held out the cherries. The boy's hands were small and tawny, like the paws of a cat; the cherries were cool in his warm palms. As he thanked Tim, the reddish spikes of the boy's hair, newly dyed and gelled, stood up, and the two older men, his housemates, who were waiting for him at the check-out counter, watched resignedly.

"Nothing to say," Garth reminded Peter.

"Eighteen years old." Peter sighed, remembering.

During the first weeks the boy had spent in their back room, sleeping on cushions in a salvaged claw-foot bathtub, Garth and Peter had tried to instill carefulness in him as they poured orange juice into glasses in the hope that he would drink, or piled individually-wrapped condoms in a handsome blue jar by the front door.

The boy did not drink the juice and, as far as they could tell, he did not avail himself of the condoms, which might mean anything, Peter thought; but Garth predicted the worst.

Now they no longer tried (although they left the handsome blue jar by the door), and even Peter, the worrier, had stopped waking up at two or three a.m. when the boy came in and threw himself—"Like a bag of cement," Garth said, although the boy was so slight; "More like a sack of eggs," Peter said—into the claw-foot bathtub.

They had insisted at the beginning that he find work. That had been their one condition after the boy's grandmother showed him the door because of who he had become. He'd had only the cash in his pocket and the clothes on his back; the two men were not prepared to support him. So the boy worked in the produce department, arranging green and yellow squash ("Beautifully," Peter said; "an innate sense of design") and spray-ing water on firm, pinkish beets, and it was there he'd met Tim, practically on the first day, the older men surmised.

Tim was at least ten years older than the boy—Peter thought fifteen—which Garth felt did not put them in a position to criticize since he was twelve years older than his lover. But they had their opinions of the situation, both shared and separate.

"We're going to give him house room, that's all," Garth had reminded Peter when they'd first found the boy on their doorstep with tears running down his cheeks.

Peter had seemed to agree, but after ten years together, Garth knew him well enough to guess that his agreement was conditional.

The boy had dried his tears and helped them heap pillows in the bathtub. It was June; he would not need blankets until September, which would mark, Garth believed, the delicately-negotiated end of his stay.

They'd actually met the boy six months earlier, hanging around the club—he was too young to be admitted, then. Coming out, the bar's customers would throw him a wave or a pat, and he, like a welcomed dog, would go wagging after them; but only Peter and Garth eventually offered him a home.

Peter had not needed to remind Garth that it had once been the same for them: the Midwest—Ohio and Indiana, respectively—the agony of school, the deepening depression and family agitation, and finally the moment of realization, which had happened for Garth in a college classroom in Columbus and for Peter in a men's room in town. Nor did they need to remind each other of the sharpness of the fresh wind that had abruptly scattered them from home and family and then landed them, like Dorothy's tornado, in Santa Fe.

When they had met at the club a few years later, Garth was already well-established in Santa Fe, and he took Peter on as an assistant and later co-owner of his flower business— Passion Fruit, it was called, which confounded some people. Since then they had prospered enough to buy the little old adobe house on Aqua Fria for which they had all kinds of long-term plans, one of which had inspired the purchase of the claw-foot bathtub. They wanted a beautiful bathroom, one day, with a giant shower and hanging ferns and finches in cages. Meantime they had the utilitarian cubicle they now shared with the boy.

There was only one note of discord in the two men's plans: they knew they would not be buried together. It could hardly be called discord, Garth thought; rather, a recognition of reality. Peter wanted to go back to his mother's family, in California (it seemed at that point they might have him), and Garth had decided to be cremated and to have Peter scatter his ashes over the Sangre de Cristo Mountains where they sometimes hiked.

Into this arrangement came the boy and then his cherries. Both men knew the cherries were not the first or the last of it, and they expected to lose their guest before long. In their experience, men who found each other did not hesitate to load up their possessions and move in together; it was essential to seize the moment and begin to forge a united front. To hesitate was to risk losing a chance at the one true place, which Garth and Peter knew they had both found, and created, with each other—the one true place from which fear was, most of the time, banished, as though a good plate of posole (Garth's specialty) or the Sunday newspaper shared on their couch could create a deeply-sunken spot where desire and pleasure and safety throve together.

The boy stepped into this spot cautiously. He treated the two men like uncles, respected and avoided them.

On the morning after the boy received his gift, Garth found what was left of the cherries in a little dish in the refrigerator. It was Monday, his day for chores, and he was tempted to throw the cherries out; they looked soft and bruised. But he knew himself well and avoided the gesture.

Later, after supper and their favorite television program, he brought the cherries out and shared them with Peter, but they tasted fermented, and both agreed it was better to let them go.

It was Garth who devised the note they left for the boy on the refrigerator shelf: THREW OUT THE REST OF YOUR CHERRIES. NOW YOU'LL HAVE AN EXCUSE TO ASK FOR MORE.

The boy didn't mention the note—he rarely opened the

refrigerator since he ate most of his meals in the supermarket, or on the run—and no more cherries appeared then in the little adobe house.

That summer, it seemed to the two men that they were waiting, as the town was waiting, for July's monsoon rains, sorely needed after six months of drought. New water restrictions (now Garth couldn't wash his '59 Chevy on the street but had to hide it in the alley for cleaning) and increasing heat were like a large screw, slowly tightening on the roof of the little adobe, which baked under its layer of dirt.

Now the scrappy neighborhood was loud with transistors and car horns and backyard parties that sometimes went on all night. When Garth would wake up, annoyed by the noise, and reach across to touch Peter, he would feel the dampness of his skin, a dampness that seemed akin to pallor, it was so light and thin. Peter did not complain about the heat or the noise, and one Saturday night when Garth suggested summoning the police to stop a very loud party next door, Peter persuaded him not to make the call.

So in addition to the screw tightening on the roof of the old adobe there was a loosening underneath it, which Garth found interesting. Peter had been the one to make most of the rules they lived by, and now he was relinquishing them not as a man in a sinking boat tosses everything overboard but as a child, flying a kite quickly, suddenly lets go of the string.

. . .

COMING HOME LATE ONE AFTERNOON in July from Passion Fruit, Garth found a pregnant tabby cat perched on the kitchen windowsill. He guessed that she was hungry and in some extremity, and he lifted the screen to let her in. After all there was more than one way of letting go of the string of the kite.

Then he filled a saucer with milk and set it in the corner for her, and she purred loudly as she lapped, then sat cleaning her whiskers. Neither he nor Peter had included pets in their life plan, but the tabby cat, as he explained to Peter later, was not really a pet but another small soul in distress, and those they would never turn away. And so the tabby was given a nest made of one of Peter's old flannel shirts, in the bottom of their closet, and the boy was given money to bring home some cans of cat food.

The food smelled bad when it was opened, and the litter box was hard to take in the hot weather, even though Garth cleaned it every day. The tabby seemed to spend an inordinate amount of time in the box, squatting and scratching, throwing gravel all over the kitchen floor. Peter was sickened by the smell. Garth said they would keep the creature only until her kittens were born and then put her out of the house.

"Have you ever seen a cat have kittens?" Peter, who had spent his summers on a farm, asked.

Garth had not. But he did not see that as a reason to avoid the experience.

The boy still went out every night, presumably with Tim. One Sunday afternoon, he brought him shyly to the DOM (dirty old men) party that had become a warm-weather tradition for the two men. The guests were indulgent to the boy and tolerated Tim; the two soon went into the bedroom to lie on the bed, eat popcorn, and look at television. And then Eleanore dropped by.

She was a six-foot-six black drag queen the two men had avoided for years because she drank too much and could become argumentative. She had not been invited to the DOM party, but she arrived as though drawn there, and went at once into the bedroom. Peter felt compelled to go in and check after a while, and he came out escorting Eleanore, who was very angry. According to the boy, she had created a scene of some sort on the madras bedspread—which explained the popcorn grease stains. The boy was astonished and embarrassed until Garth and Peter laughed it off. (Tim, leaving abruptly, was notably silent.) After all, what was there to forgive? Eleanore had been drawn there and had behaved as she always behaved, drunk or sober, and the only consequence was a trip to the washing machine for the madras spread.

In fact both men liked the way the boy was introducing an element of uncertainty into their lives.

On July Fourth the tabby cat gave birth while Garth and Peter were at a barbecue in Tesuque. When they came back, their bedroom smelled rank; in the closet, the tabby was licking up a pool of blood and mucous. Six wormlike creatures lay wrapped in membrane.

Peter took one look and began to retch (in spite of his farm background, Garth thought with satisfaction), and it was left to the older man to clean things up. In five minutes he was outside the house taking deep breaths of cooling evening air, and the tabby was still at her labors. It was several hours before the closet was cleaned and the kittens cleared of their membranes; when the two men looked in again, near midnight, the scene was more idyllic.

"So when are you throwing her out?" Peter asked when they were in bed.

"As soon as those kittens are weaned."

Two of the kittens were dead in the morning, and Peter, heroically, Garth thought, volunteered to dispose of them. They both had the impression, based on the tabby's expression, that she might eat the corpses if given a chance.

The boy was just coming in from his night out and he stood in the doorway, watching Peter on his knees in the closet, extracting the corpses from the hissing mother. The boy seemed bewildered.

Both men felt exhausted by the experience and almost unwilling to discuss it.

The summer was fast rising to its peak, and still there was

not enough rain; now they limited their showers to a minute each and insisted that the boy do the same, which caused a problem. But eventually he complied after they explained, patiently, that they all drew from the same aquifer and must work to preserve it.

Privately, Garth thought the boy believed water arrived on earth in plastic containers bought at the supermarket. He did not seem to have a clear sense of causes, or of consequences, which reminded Garth of the very young Peter, with his smooth chin and neck, glancing around the club those first nights years ago. It had taken Peter several years to realize that even in Santa Fe, he and Garth did not swing in a vacuum but swam in the same river as everyone else, even if moved along by a separate current.

Late in July the boy was laid off from his job for reasons he did not choose to discuss but which apparently had to do with a rift with Tim. Garth was quietly sympathetic—he knew what it was to lose work and relationship together—and soon offered him a job at Passion Fruit.

The boy learned the ropes quickly and was quite helpful with the customers, especially the women, whom he enjoyed charming. He did have an innate sense of design, as Peter had said at the beginning, and was soon able to put together simple arrangements for birthday parties or hospital visits. These were not the sort of arrangements Garth and Peter specialized in—in fact, if they could have afforded to they would have discouraged those clients—and so they were grateful for the boy's limited and conventional expertise. He was even able to make a vase of red gladioli look a little less like a quiver of exposed weapons.

In August, Garth began to take a Spanish class at the community college, which was an item on his list of goals; he wanted to learn Spanish, to play the piano, and to sing the ballads of his childhood before he turned fifty. And fifty was fast approaching. Peter encouraged him to take time off from the shop now that the boy was able to absorb some of the slack, and Garth went quite willingly.

He was usually back by closing time. Sometimes when he came in the shop, Peter and the boy were laughing, or leaning together on the counter, going over accounts. Their hands were similar, Garth noticed, small and tawny and pawlike, although of course Peter's were more firmly molded. They greeted him quietly and pleasantly, and after locking up, all three walked home together, telling the stories of their day. Now Garth had new details to add from his Spanish class, which was full of characters.

As soon as they were back in the house, Peter would begin to put together dinner. Now that Tim was no longer in the picture, the boy often ate with them, and he had volunteered to take on the care of the tabby and her kittens, including dealing with the foul-smelling food cans and the even fouler-smelling litter box.

The kittens, at six weeks, were joyful and accomplished charmers, climbing up into the men's laps and playing with their fingers, leaping and batting and mewing while the tabby looked on tolerantly. There was no more talk of getting rid of them.

In August the rains finally came and the house's gutters brimmed and overflowed nearly every afternoon; rainwater ran straight down the windows. It was important to remember to close up in the morning, and to lay rags along the sills since the old wooden frames were warped and no longer fit. Even so, there was often water on the floors when they came home.

One afternoon when the rains had held off and Peter and the boy had decided to take in a movie, Garth came home alone. He was seldom on his own in the little house; it was a luxury he relished. The kittens were playing on the figured carpet in the living room—one of the few household items sent on by Peter's family—and a ray of sunlight fell over them from the rain-washed window.

Garth stood in the doorway, admiring them. Their small striped bodies flexed and leaped, their white paws batted the air, and one little gray one lay alone on her side, luxuriating in the sunlight. Garth stood for a long time, watching.

He was in bed reading when Peter and the boy came home; he heard their voices in the living room and thought of getting up. Some time later, after he had fallen asleep, Peter came in, undressed, and got into bed. Garth reached across and took his hand.

In the morning Garth was the first one up, as often happened now; he went into the kitchen to start the coffee. A stained, brown paper bag sagged in the middle of the kitchen table. It was half full of cherry stems and pits that still looked wet. Garth allowed himself to throw the bag out.

He was disturbed that day as he had not been in some time, and he tried to let the waves of disturbance carry him easily. He knew from long experience that there was no way to fight disturbance, to control or overcome it, and he also knew it would pass, in its own time, like all pain.

He went to his Spanish class in the afternoon and sat there numbly, because even though he would learn nothing it was important to keep to the smallest detail of their routine.

Later, when he went by the shop, he found that Peter and the boy had closed up early, leaving a note to tell him that things had been slow and they had decided to take the afternoon off and go swimming.

They did not invite him to join them. Garth knew that if they had, he would not have followed them.

He went home quietly. In the house, the kittens were

playing on the rug, and he stood for a long time, watching them. Then he reheated posole left from the weekend, ate a little, and went to bed early. To his surprise, he had no difficulty in falling asleep, and he did not wake up, much later, when Peter came in.

It seemed that now they were moving separately, like the branches of one tree stirred by different breaths of wind.

A few mornings later, Garth got up without disturbing Peter—it was very early—and went into the living room. The light through the rain-washed windows was new and fresh, and it flashed off bowls and baskets of cherries, set on every surface.

Garth walked among them. Here was his grandmother's Ming bowl, brimming with cherries, and a little basket from the state fair, also filled to overflowing. A Fiestaware vase was crammed with them, and the crystal goblet he'd given Peter on their first anniversary was stuffed to the brim. In the fresh early light the cherries winked and shone, as though, Garth thought, they would glow and pulsate even in the dark.

The house was very quiet.

He went into the kitchen and began to fill the percolator. There were more cherries there, too, in the yellow mixing bowl, even in the blender. Peter must have bought pounds and pounds of them, Garth thought. On the kitchen table there was a small pile of stems and pits which someone had herded together carefully.

After a while, Garth made himself some toast. Peter came in then, and the boy soon after him, in bare feet, yawning, wearing his pajama bottoms; he still had a child's soft, slack stomach, Garth noticed, pouching out over the drawstring.

They sat around the kitchen table, drinking coffee and eating toast and cherries.

Garth reminded himself that with Peter he had found, for the first time, the true place. The deed to the little house was in both their names, and the life they had made there was in both their names, as well.

He stirred the pile of cherry stems and pits with his finger and watched the red stains spread on the white table. On the other side, the boy was drinking his coffee, and Peter was quietly watching.

"It's time the boy had a bed," Garth said. He felt the edges of each word; they were sharp, yet they did not cut. "Even the tabby has her own bed, now"—an expensive pet-store basket with plaid cushion.

Peter said nothing. He went on looking at Garth. The boy began to whistle.

With some rearrangement of the furniture, there was room in the living room for a single bed, which could be disguised as a sofa with throw pillows and a spread. In the end they decided to cover it with the madras bedspread that had once been soiled by popcorn grease. Peter said he had never really liked it, and it seemed appropriate that it would go to Garth, who treasured it.

Garth moved into the living room the next evening, after work, leaving most of his clothes in the bedroom Peter would now share with the boy.

The cherries stayed in their bowls and baskets and vases all week. Now and then one of the men would scoop up a cherry and eat it, discarding stem and pit carelessly.

Finally the house began to smell of fermented juice, and Peter threw out all the cherries and washed the containers. He lined up vases and baskets and bowls beside the sink to dry. Garth, sitting in the living room, heard Peter whistling and looked at the kittens playing on the rug.

The Big Bed

Heading, as always, toward adventure, Liz wanted, the summer she turned sixty-four, to pass through unconditional love (which she had barely achieved—for the world, for Oliver, for her dog, Sam) to what appeared to be its inevitable other side: transgression.

She had taken so many risks in her life that sometimes she felt their more or less dreadful consequences must have worn away her privilege. Money continued to flow into her checking account from her grandfather's mines in Colorado, or rather from the investments he'd made, prudently, when the mines were forced to close; but the protection that money had once conferred was gone.

Now Liz lived as many other people lived, in a small old house in a Southwestern town, with a fenced yard for Sam, who ran back and forth, supervising the neighborhood, his tail as rigid as a ruler, and a big, shady bed where Oliver usually spent the weekend, recovering from his job as a high-school history teacher.

It was the big bed that turned Liz to thinking about transgression. The frame was dark mahogany, so high Liz had to slide out of it as though she was sliding down a hill, and climb back up with one leg cocked to hip level to make the grade; the bed had been in the family and was passed down to her because no one else wanted it. The pineapples carved at the top of the tall posts symbolized, she'd been told, hospitality.

Oliver, who'd led a different life in a different place with a woman he called "my friend," began one Sunday morning to talk about fantasies. Liz was instantly alerted, as though by the smell of something burning.

"Once I actually had a fantasy," Oliver told her. "I mean, it actually happened."

They were lying on their backs after lovemaking, warm in the late-morning sun, her thigh across his. Liz asked him to go on.

(Later, she would think that was the turning point, coming as it usually did without warning or premeditation: the moment when she asked Oliver to go on.)

"My friend had a woman friend, and she came for a visit,"

he began, leaning up on one elbow, his bearded, leonine face hovering over her, like Jehovah's. "The friend was plain, dumpy, the kind of woman who has trouble finding a man.

"We were in bed that night, and she came through the hall on her way to the bathroom. Our door was open."

"Who left it open?" Liz asked.

"We just didn't bother to close it. We didn't worry much about that kind of thing since we were nearly always alone in the house. Anyway, she came in, to tell my friend good night, and then she just stood there, looking at us so wistfully. Both of us reached out at the same time and drew her in.

"It was ecstasy, for me," he said, and she saw the high, pale shine on his face. "My friend gave me to her."

Liz felt something stir in the place Oliver had recently filled. "What happened next day?" she asked.

"The friend left. Later on," he added softly, "she found a man. We both thought there was a connection. I mean, she'd felt loved, maybe for the first time."

Liz unwound herself from him and went to the bathroom. Leaning on the sink, she studied her face in the mirror. Long trained by introspection, she knew how to interpret her gaunt look. She splashed water on her face as though to dilute her expression. One of her demons, the little one who laughed sarcastically, winked out of her reflection, then disappeared as though in haste to be gone.

Oliver was waiting for her. "I shouldn't have told you that."

"I'm glad you did."

"But something's wrong." He reached for her, and she caught his hand.

"I want to give you everything," Liz said.

LIZ'S FRIENDS, WHO KNEW HER HISTORY, would have warned her immediately of the danger, had they known. To have a fantasy is one thing; to act on it, another. Liz's fantasy sprouted in the soft summer air along with all the other seedling hopes and dreams that had followed her out of childhood. Courage and money had planted many in reality, where they had grown into their native shapes, twisted or flowing. This particular fantasy had already sprouted a long, hairy root.

She knew immediately whom she would ask: her plain, adorable friend Patty. Long divorced and retired, immersed in volunteer work and grandchildren, Patty presented to the world the bright face of resignation. But Liz knew her well—knew her late-night bleakness, her episodes of self-gnawing despair.

The only question, really, was how to approach her. Patty wasn't a conventional woman—none of Liz's friends were—but she was squeamish. Once on a hike she'd shuddered at the sight of a black snake, sunning itself on the trail. So Liz planned her invitation carefully.

Over lunch under a green-and-white umbrella, in one of the cafes that catered to locals, Liz solicited Patty's help. "There's something I want to do for Oliver, and I can't do it alone."

She recognized her friend's alerted look, the slight widening of the eyes and drooping of the lower lip that signaled a break in ordinary smoothness, the smoothness of two women drinking herbal iced tea under a green-and-white umbrella.

"What is it, Liz?" Patty asked.

"It's a fantasy he told me about, that actually happened, once, and meant a great deal to him," Liz said, choosing her words with care. "The woman he was living with at the time gave him to a friend of hers, for one night."

"You mean just loaned him out?"

They smiled at each other, fellow travelers in the rugged country of love.

"No, they were together in bed, all three of them."

Patty drew a breath and looked away. Liz drank some iced tea. Next to her, on the retaining wall, a trailing nasturtium was opening big oval leaves to the sun.

"But I know Oliver, a little," Patty said. Her hand, turning her iced-tea glass, was carefully manicured, Liz noticed, decorated with her old engagement ring, its small diamond as bright, still, as it would have been forty years ago when both of them thought they wanted such rings.

"You've met him a few times. I wouldn't say you know him.

And unless you wanted to, you wouldn't have to meet him again," Liz said, remembering the few occasions, rather awkward, when she'd invited old friends to inspect Oliver over a cheese omelet and tomato salad.

"But he wouldn't want me," Patty murmured.

Now Liz felt the edge of her opportunity. "That's the whole point. He wants to give himself, briefly, to a woman who doesn't believe she is lovable."

Patty glanced at her, troubled. The memory of their late-night talks was darkening her cheerful, sensible face. Her strong, freckled forearm, lying along the white tablecloth, quivered.

"And you can be certain there would be no consequences," added Liz.

As she was paying for their tea, she remembered that in the story Oliver had told her, there had been a consequence—at least one, of which she knew.

After that it would have been easy for Liz to believe it was just a question of arrangements, as deaths and marriages can be transformed, at some point, into a question of arrangements. Calendars had to be consulted—everyone, of course, was very busy, retirement or the absence of work did not mean more free time—and a few telephone calls went to advise Patty about what she should wear (something simple, and loose) and what she should bring (her toothbrush, hormonal cream, etc.). Liz recognized during these calls, which she did not make in Oliver's presence, that she was quietly reassuring her friend, who moved in the space of a few days from jubilant anticipation to stoical fear. Her fear was not, Liz realized, that she would be shamed by the exposure but rather that she would be rejected—thrown out of their covenant as being, for obscure reasons, unworthy. Without precisely intending to, Liz realized she had touched the nub of her friend's anxiety. Immediately, she grew fonder of her.

In the days before the evening they'd agreed on, Liz thought of Patty's body, plump and strong, the body of a woman who split her own kindling. Liz had never seen her friend naked, but she had perceived the powerful shape of her body under the rather shapeless clothes she ordinarily wore. However, Patty's body, like all bodies except Oliver's, had not meant anything to Liz other than the necessary connection between her friend's feet, hands, and head. She did not remember even noticing whether Patty wore perfume, or whether her skin was cool or warm to the touch.

She prevented herself from telling Oliver about the present, as she had decided to call it, until the day before the event was to occur.

"I've arranged a little present for you," she said then. "A treat, really."

He was used to her small, exquisite treats—a monogrammed

silk pocket-handkerchief, an old-fashioned fountain pen. Now he smiled, already halfway to appreciation. "What have you cooked up now?" It had become a joke between them that she was the present-giver, the treat-concocter, and that both of them were perfectly comfortable with the arrangement. Oliver was a good receiver, which was one of the reasons Liz loved him.

"I'm going to loan you," she said.

He looked at her with glistening attention, but said nothing.

"I've invited Patty to come over tomorrow night."

"Patty. Patty." The name, she could tell, meant nothing.

"You've met her a couple of times. You probably don't remember her. There's no need to know anything about her. She's not beautiful," she added, with a little, demonic grin. "But then that would spoil it."

She could see him making the necessary link. "A woman who doesn't feel lovable."

"Yes," she said. "That's the way I've explained it to her."

One of the delights of being with Oliver was that he required few amplifications; now, it was enough that he was going to receive something from Liz, something she had chosen with her usual care. He reached across the table and took her hand. "I love you," he said, and knowing that the words only rose to his lips on a tide of feeling, Liz was, in her turn, swept by reciprocal delight. The shared feeling was as warm, and as soft, as the late-afternoon breeze that lifted the ends of her hair and stirred the daisies that hung their limp necks over the vase in the middle of the table.

"I love you, too," she said, grateful that they spoke those words so seldom. Love, after all, existed not in words but in their daily connection—the exhausted, often nearly-mute telephone conversations late at night, the grind of his tires on the gravel outside her little house, the way he waved backward out of the window when he drove away. In the old days, Liz knew, a chorus of demons would have feasted on those scant details, reminding her in their shrill, clever voices that she saw Oliver only on weekends, that they did not really share a life together. The demons had almost been silenced, six months before, when Liz had felt her first true flow of feeling, spooning chicken soup into Oliver's mouth when he was down with the flu, seeing the translucent gloss of fever on his high forehead. It was the first time he had come to her in helplessness and need. It would not be the last.

Aware of the dangers inherent in special occasions, Liz didn't let herself cook a company dinner on Friday. Instead, she limited herself to a simple pasta dish with homemade tomato sauce, lenient on the garlic, and a cucumber salad.

Patty arrived a few minutes late, and there was a moment of awkwardness when she hesitated in the doorway, her doll-sized suitcase in hand. Then Oliver hurried forward and took the suitcase, ushering her into the kitchen where the round maple table was set with three white mats.

"Welcome," he said. Liz breathed deeply. She had never heard him use that word before.

Patty beamed. "It smells so good in here!"

"That's the basil in my sauce—it's from my garden," Liz said, as she stirred at the stove. "Why don't you cut up the cucumbers?"

The two women stood side by side in the honey-colored light that fell through the west-facing window; Liz tasted her sauce—it was perfect, from long years of practice—and poured it into the white china bowl of green spaghetti. At the same time, Patty scooped her paper-thin cucumber slices into the wooden salad bowl that had come to Liz with her first marriage. Oliver was lighting the candles in the pressed-tin holders that stood in the middle of the maple table.

After much admonishment, Sam settled with a groan on his patch of carpet.

"I'm going to say grace," Liz said as they took their places. She had never thought of such a thing before.

Obediently, the other two bowed their heads, but not before Oliver had shot her a curious glance. They were both involved in a spiritual practice that had nothing to do with churches.

Liz tried to remember ritual words from her childhood, from proper Thanksgivings, but they didn't come to her. "Gratitude for all these good things," she murmured at last. "Amen."

The others murmured "Amen" with her. She knew she was grateful for more than the food on the table, and she felt quite sure that both Patty and Oliver were grateful for a wider range of gifts, as well. And the greatest of these, she thought, paraphrasing a passage from Corinthians, is courage.

For what, after all, she thought, is the use of age if it doesn't bring us to courage? She felt the edge, as though with her finger, of its connection to her concept of love.

They ate slowly, drinking a few sips of wine, talking of nothing consequential. Patty had just returned from a visit to her newest grandchild; she'd actually been in the delivery room when the baby was born. She was excited about that, but calmer than usual, as though even that unexpected experience had achieved its proper proportion. Oliver talked of his grown son, who was prospering as a lawyer in L.A. Liz had no children to add to the congenial stew. She ate and smiled, utterly contented, utterly at home in her warm kitchen.

Afterward they cleaned up together, and Oliver gave Sam some scraps, which he accepted greedily. Patty insisted on sponging down the wooden counters.

Then they sat for a while on the porch with their mugs of

decaffeinated coffee. The stars were coming out in the blurred summer sky; Oliver pointed to several constellations. Liz knew that each named star, as it emerged from the dusty sky, was charged with administering her destiny. The need to fix, to make happen—even to move—fell from her like a heavy winter coat. She sat on the old, hard-hipped bench—another survivor of marriage—with her thighs apart, her bare feet resting on Oliver's knee, her cotton skirt drifting to one side.

Patty, stretched out in the lounge chair, slid her pretty, manicured feet out of her sandals. Only Oliver, laced into his sneakers, remained shod.

Their voices drifted, then twined together. The words had no particular import. Now and then they glanced at each other, in the failing light, with mute reassurance, like passengers in a lifeboat rowing steadily for the shore.

"Let's go up," Oliver said at ten, and he went around the little house, as usual, locking doors and windows. Liz and Patty walked upstairs with Sam padding along behind them.

"You use the bathroom first, I'm going to unpack," Patty said, an unfamiliar note of command in her pleasant voice. Liz, relieved, obeyed. She had no further need, or wish, to orchestrate the evening. Even Sam seemed to understand; he lay down quietly on his pad in the corner of her bedroom and went to sleep.

In her best blue nightgown, Liz lay in the big bed, waiting.

Around her, the house slowly quieted. Oliver closed a window downstairs, and she imagined his long fingers snapping the lock. In the bathroom, Patty hummed a fragment of a show tune and ran water into the sink. After a while, Liz heard her open the bathroom door and walk down the hall to her room. She imagined that her friend's freshly-washed feet were leaving small, shapely footprints on the wooden floor.

Oliver went into the bathroom next, and, with his usual efficiency, was out of his clothes and ready for bed in five minutes. He came softly into the bedroom and turned out all the lamps except the one they customarily left on, in the corner. It threw shadows high up onto the bare wooden walls, peopling the room, Liz felt, with watchers.

Oliver climbed into bed beside her and took her in his arms. Liz felt, with her palm, the steady warmth of his erection.

"That happened fast," she said with a contented laugh.

"Yes," he said. "I like my present already. You made a good choice."

"She's never been fulfilled," Liz said.

"And yet she's not especially needy," Oliver commented.

"Not enough to frighten either one of us," Liz agreed.

They waited. The house clicked with the small mechanical sounds of kitchen appliances settling into dormancy. The shadows on the walls grew softer, thicker, and seemed to exude a scent, like shaggy pines after a rain.

At last—and whether it had been a long wait or a short one, Liz didn't know, or care—they heard Patty's footsteps in the hall. She looked in their open door.

"I came to say good night," she said; she and Liz had agreed that would be the cue.

"Come in." As Oliver turned his head, Liz felt his beard brush her breast.

Patty came to the side of the bed. She was wearing a sensible calico robe. Oliver reached out, and, at that moment, Liz reached out as well. Together, they unknotted the sash and Patty, with a sigh, stepped out of the robe and let it fall around her naked feet.

Her body, in the dim light, was whiter and shapelier than Liz had imagined, and she felt a pang of fear. Then she reached out and touched her friend's thigh, pressing her palm against the bunched flesh. "Come in," she said as Oliver lifted the sheet.

Like a tired child, Patty slid into the bed beside them. Oliver tucked the sheet securely around her. For a moment they all lay on their backs, staring at the shadowed ceiling.

Then Oliver turned, letting go of Liz, and touched Patty's big, rosy nipple.

"I love you very much," Liz said to his gleaming back. She could feel his industry, his determination, and it made her smile as once she might have smiled at a beloved child wreaking havoc with shovel and pail in a sandbox.

Her calm continued, a satin ribbon winding around the three bodies, under the arms, between the legs, softly noosing the necks. She had expected excitement, even frenzy, but what she felt as her friend made her secret sounds of satisfaction was simply peace.

When Oliver was assured that both women were satisfied, he fell asleep with his head on Liz's breast.

Some time before dawn, Patty got out of bed and stole away. Liz, half-waking, appreciated her delicacy; Patty did not feel it was necessary, or appropriate, to witness the lovers' waking.

They did not eat breakfast together. They did not eat at all; although later, Liz heard Oliver in the kitchen, feeding Sam and making coffee. She lay dozing in the big bed, feeling her stomach and thighs, which seemed heavier, more developed than they'd been before. Now and then, she softly stroked her nipples, so much smaller and darker than her friend's.

She heard Patty come down the hall about ten o'clock. She stopped in the doorway, and Liz saw she had her little suitcase in hand.

"Thank you," she said.

"You are very welcome."

Patty went downstairs. Liz heard Oliver greet her with affection in the kitchen. A few minutes later, the front door closed and a car started. Liz dozed until Oliver came in with her coffee.

He sat on the edge of the big bed and watched her drink. Liz was naked, her long, dull hair spread over her shoulders. Her small nipples grazed the edge of the sheet.

"That was ecstasy, for me," Oliver said.

Later—years later—when Oliver had gone (and that was after they had both met Patty's young man—the young man she'd had dinner with a week after the gift), Liz wondered if Oliver's long-ago friend, in that other city, had hoped to bind him closer with her generosity. Oliver was a wanderer, after all, a man who even now, in late middle age, possessed the energy to leave any situation. He had left Liz one morning quickly and calmly, with no explanation—and no explanation had been needed.

Later, Liz began to see the pointed face of one of her old demons. He asked her, in his high, spiteful voice that was full of cleverness and bile, whether she, too, had hoped to hold Oliver by offering Patty to him.

She was not able, then, to answer the demon's question. She was in pain, and pain tended to confuse her.

A year or so later, when she was cutting up basil for spaghetti sauce, she looked at the scissors in her hand and remembered the meal they had cooked together that night, and how Patty, even on the edge of illumination, had sliced the cucumbers paper-thin.

Stanley

S tanley lived in the barrio on the west side of Santa Fe because he couldn't afford to live on the east side, where most of his friends rented apartments or even houses. He was a draftsman, working for the city, and that meant, he knew, that he might never be able to live on the east side and invite his friends to dinner in a rustic kitchen with exposed beams.

His two rooms on Bacca Street were a little dark, and since he had an artist's eye, this troubled him, especially when he woke early on a spring morning and noticed that almost no light penetrated the tiny windows.

But the office was where he spent most of his daylight hours, and it was bright and high-ceilinged, filled with the goings-and-comings of a large staff; they were especially busy that year because of the water shortage which made all new building more or less problematical, and the legal problems that arose every time a contractor was refused a permit.

Stanley was preoccupied at times with anxieties about his significance; he was the only child of a devoted mother, and he was used to being the appropriate as well as the only vehicle of her expectations. She expected, and always would expect, great things.

After he had been in Santa Fe for five years, she began to ask about his friends rather than his job, and he understood that she no longer thought his profession offered much hope of advancement. She wanted him to marry; he was thirty-nine and had never met anyone who seemed entirely right.

"But I'm not lonely," he told her.

"I know you have a lot of friends, but that's not the same thing. Think about when I'm gone—when you'll be old."

"I like the way I live," he told her. "Why should I change it?"

When he returned to his two rooms on Bacca Street after an evening spent with friends, he would notice with pleased surprise that the few objects he had managed to accumulate had a certain style: his bed was disguised as a plain white couch, and his pillows and soft blue blanket were kept in a painted chest. His walls were bare except for four quite remarkable black-and-white photographs of the desert given to him, rather surprisingly, by an acquaintance.

He'd had no reason to expect a gift from this woman. They'd spent several pleasant evenings at the houses of mutual acquaintances, and once they'd gone on a hike, which had been spoiled by the behavior of her dog; Stanley had decided he would not hike with her again. Once he'd invited her to a movie and dinner, but the dinner turned out to be more expensive than he'd expected, and Maria had failed to volunteer to split the bill.

Whenever he looked at the photographs, Stanley felt both slightly uneasy and satisfied, as though he'd eaten something rich that mildly disagreed with him. Sometimes he imagined telling his mother that his room was decorated with four fine photographs that were gifts from a woman he knew; he realized, though, that his mother would want to know who she was.

One evening in the spring, he noticed Maria sitting in the corner of the coffee shop where he always bought his lattée, her long brown hair hanging down in two folds, almost covering her face. She was writing something in a handsome leather-bound notebook.

On impulse, he carried his cup to her table and sat down. She closed her notebook quickly and looked up with a smile.

"I've been meaning to ask you about those photographs you gave me," he said. "Who took them?"

"I did," she said, looking surprised.

"I didn't know you were a photographer."

"Why, what did you think I was?"

Stanley realized he'd never given the question any thought.

"Do you think I spend my time going to dinner parties?" she asked, still smiling, but with a fixed expression.

"Nothing the matter with dinner parties," he said, "especially if you like to feast on bones." They started on some rather satisfactory gossip: one of the group was about to be divorced–"A lot of marrow there," Stanley said. Pleased by her appetite for this kind of thing–friendship, after all, should never be allowed to dull wit–he found himself asking if she would be free to go to a concert of Spanish guitar music.

She agreed, quickly, to go with him, and he wondered for an instant whether he could ask her to pay for her ticket.

That evening when his mother called, Stanley told her he had a date with an attractive woman, and she seemed pleased. Later, he remembered that he'd wanted to go to the concert alone; but he decided that no harm could come from sitting beside Maria, listening to music.

They met on the steps of the auditorium, which was modeled on a Spanish church. Inside, a busy throng was crowding into the pewlike seats, and Maria pushed her own way in, creating a path for Stanley. He admired her broad shoulders and long neck, and appreciated that she was wearing what looked like silk pants.

Maria was a restless listener, and her stirrings irritated Stanley. Either she was shifting the program on her knee—once she actually dropped it—or she was rearranging herself, moving closer to him. He became unpleasantly aware of the heat of her thigh, pressing against his. Only the appearance of the guitarist, with his long black hair and full mustache, modified his discomfort.

"How about coming to my house for a drink?" Maria asked when the concert was over.

Stanley accepted, thinking this would give him an opportunity to ask about her photography, perhaps to find out more about the prints she'd given him.

Maria's living room was attractively gotten up with what he recognized as English chintz. There was a piano in the corner, and he would have liked to ask her if she played, but he felt uneasy about revealing his ignorance of the details of her life.

After a few glasses of wine, Maria stood up, yawning, and began to unbutton her shirt. Stanley saw she had nothing on underneath.

"I need to go home," he said.

She seemed genuinely surprised. "Don't you like me?"

"Of course I do," Stanley said, as though that would end the conversation, and he stood up.

"You always sit next to me at parties," she said. Her breasts were quite visible inside the open shirt, and Stanley thought they were well-shaped.

"It's not the same thing," he said, moving away from her. "You see, I want to get married and start a family."

"I'm thirty-five," she said.

He had assumed she was too old—she looked at least five years older than he was—and now he was speechless with confusion. Perhaps nothing he knew about her was accurate; perhaps he was only able to see her through a sort of scrim. He found himself saying that it wasn't only a question of age.

She came closer, and he smelled the light lemony fragrance she always wore, and understood that since he recognized it, he must have stood or sat in close proximity to her often before.

"I didn't know you were so conventional," she said, laying a hand on his arm.

He looked down at her pink fingernails. "I'm not conventional," he said. It was a word his mother used. "But I do know what I want."

"Then leave. Don't come sidling up to me the next time we run into each other," she said, withdrawing her hand.

He left, feeling humiliated and angry. What had he done

to merit such a rejection? Now he knew there would be an awkwardness whenever he encountered her; he would dread the occasion beforehand, and feel constrained during it, and torment himself with analysis afterward. It might be better, he thought, simply to give up the social life he had carefully constructed.

When he went back to his little house on Bacca Street, he saw the four photographs glaring out of the darkness, and he took them down hastily and stored them in his closet.

Brushing his teeth, it occurred to him that they might be worth something. If so, he could sell them and use the money for camping equipment.

He needed to know, from Maria, how to value the photographs, and this seemed a legitimate way to work himself back into what would seem, at least, to be a normal acquaintance. So when they met a week later, at a Salsa party, Stanley walked up to her (never, he knew would he *sidle*), greeted her politely, and said, "I wonder if you could tell me approximately what those photographs are worth. It's a question of my insurance," he added when he saw her expression.

She turned on her heel and walked away.

Stanley was discomfited but he was also, he realized, pleased. A curious smile lit up his face and twisted the corners of his mouth, and a woman he knew only slightly came up and claimed his attention as though she had been waiting for a while.

There are plenty more fish in the sea, his mother used to say.

Stanley found himself wanting that twitch of satisfaction again. He did not find it in his ordinary life; when he tried saying something unexpected to his co-workers, they did not respond as he wished, and the whole thing fell flat.

He remembered now that he had enjoyed teasing his mother, when he was ten or eleven, keeping it up until her ability to humor him was exhausted and she told him, sharply, to stop. He remembered making remarks about her dyed hair and her make-up and the way she put cotton between her toes before painting her nails. His mother was a serious woman, a teacher at the local junior college, and she did not much like the use Stanley made of her private indulgences. Still, he'd kept on, dancing around her like a mischievous sprite, until adolescence took him and he lost interest.

Now, it seemed to him, the pleasure he derived from teasing was essential to his life; and the best way to that pleasure was, clearly, Maria. She was easily discomfited, and he intended to profit from her weakness.

He began going up to her whenever he saw her at a social gathering, or getting her lattée and newspaper at the neighborhood cafe. He knew she was unable to defend herself, although she tried several devices: avoiding him by rushing out the door, sneering at him, refusing to speak, but always her pale face took on a haunted expression when she saw him approaching.

He teased her about the photographs—had she spent many days, camped out in the desert? Like O'Keeffe, did she wear a black cloak and wide-brimmed hat—about her piano playing, which he claimed disturbed the neighbors; he told her what their friends said about her, always prefacing each remark with, "I think you'd want to know," and he smiled indulgently at her pastel-colored silk clothes which, he told her, would look great on Madison Avenue.

His remarks were broad and even coarse, he realized—they had to be, since he knew so little about her—but like blows from a thick stick, they achieved their purpose, and he saw that she was beginning to be a little afraid of him.

This could be done to anyone, he realized. All that was needed was to break a silent agreement.

Maria began to look older that winter, and he wondered if she had lied to him about her age. There was something gaunt about her now, as though she was recovering from a long illness, and her fair skin looked yellow.

In January, other people began to intrude, and Stanley realized that Maria was complaining.

The first was the husband of a woman who'd once asked Stanley to invite them to his house; his name was Fred something, and he was an architect, rather well-off.

He called Stanley at the office and asked awkwardly if they could meet for a cup of coffee; out of a perverse fascination with serendipity, Stanley chose the neighborhood cafe where he still occasionally saw Maria.

Stanley was already seated at one of the tables when Fred came in, and he stood up as though to welcome him. But as he smiled and held out his hand, Stanley felt apprehensive, skittish even, as though Fred knew a secret.

He didn't, as it turned out, but he did tell Stanley that Maria was considering taking out a restraining order against him; she'd told Fred and his wife (Helen? Helena?) that Stanley was harassing her.

Stanley flushed and took a gulp of his lattée. "Why are women so sensitive?" he grumbled. "Even a horse lets you look in its eyes, and that's about all I did." Fred left, somewhat hurriedly.

It was Helen (Helena?) who'd sent Fred on this mission, Stanley knew. Neither one of them had ever given him the time of day, before; he was an extra man, to be invited to large parties but denied real intimacy. Now, they saw him for who and what he was. And he saw them for who they were—meddlers, professional sympathizers with women.

After that, other people in their circle whom he'd known only slightly—a name, but not the correct one, a gesture, an expression—began to loom up, as though emerging from a mist. All of them had something to say to him, with looks if not with words, and none of them had had anything to say to him, before.

"Am I your hobby?" Stanley asked one of them—an unctuous gray-haired woman who'd been trying to get him to read a book.

"You need to understand what you're doing to Maria," she said severely, waving the book at him; it was called something like, *Why Men Don't Feel.*

"What if I know what I'm doing?"

"Then surely you'd stop," she said, suddenly uneasy, and then, as he continued to smile, she turned away.

Meanwhile the city was cutting back; rumors floated around the department about a considerable downsizing. Stanley knew there were too many draftsmen.

The next time his mother called, he was a little sharp with her. She didn't telephone for two weeks, and he missed her.

The following day, a woman named Susan Trent called to beg him—that was her verb—to leave Maria alone. She asked Stanley if he was aware of the difficulties Maria regularly encountered due to her Hispanic background.

Stanley was astonished and then gratified, as though he'd known this well-kept secret all along. It gave his pursuit of Maria a cultural dimension.

When his mother finally called again, he found himself inventing a story for her. It was late afternoon of the day when he'd received his notice of termination; it was also a day when he'd surprised Maria, buying a bunch of jonquils in front of the supermarket, and she'd fled, stumbling through the ranks of parked cars.

"I think I've finally met the right woman," he told his mother, and he answered her delighted questions with every detail he could invent about his intended.

The Pump

All day the man in the knee pads and cowboy hat has been working at pulling my old pump out of the well. My old pump has died and my house has no water, and so Mike's activity—his name is Mike Boyd—is of great interest to me. The kitchen sink is full of dirty dishes and the washing machine is piled with dirty clothes and this is not the way I want to live; Mike has promised me that he will have the old pump uprooted and hauled away and the new pump installed by five o'clock this afternoon.

But it is already nearly one, and the old pump has not yet emerged from its hiding place deep in the narrow, dark well. The well was driven down into the rock of this mountain eighteen years ago; no wells have been allowed here since, because the aquifer is nearly depleted. My pump is one of several that was grandfathered in by the city council, and so it seems to me to have particular status, like an elderly person protected from violence by a police order.

Mike's work is hard, noisy, and slow. From my studio window, I peer out at him now and again, trying to assess his progress. It is difficult to tell how much he has accomplished since he drove his big white truck through my back gate two hours ago, parked it beside my wellhead (the well, although deep, is amazingly narrow, stoppered by a steel cap no bigger than a garbage-can top), and set up a large beach umbrella.

Under the umbrella, Mike and two children I assume are his grandsons are staging a delicate choreography, having to do with a big reel of metal cable. The cable unspools little by little from the reel, with a grinding noise, and as it unspools, Mike, from the shade of his umbrella, guides it down into the well with a gloved hand. His grandsons stand on either side, ready to hand Mike a tool when one is needed.

After a few feet of the metal cable have descended into the well, the grinding stops and Mike surveys the situation.

I am watching closely because this is a matter of some importance to me—last night I had to wash my hair, most unsatisfactorily, in the kitchen sink with a bottle of bought water—but also because my preoccupation with Mike and the well makes me less likely to break down and call my lover.

Tom has not been with me long enough, really, to earn that title; we came together two weeks ago on a night when neither of us expected anything to happen, after a lackluster party. We are both in our early sixties, and a wasted evening weighs a good deal more on us now than it would have thirty years ago.

Thirty years ago, we might have made love on my white linen couch without expecting much to come of it, other than a few decencies of affection and a follow-up phone call to ensure that no harm had been done. But that was a long time ago, when one encounter with a man seemed to lead inevitably to another encounter with a different man, days or weeks later, and so there was really no such thing as loss. It was a childish way to deal with relationships, I suppose, as though each one possessed no more intrinsic value than a violet gumdrop—and melted as quickly and as sweetly on the tongue.

Of course Tom and I are different now. We've both lived through long marriages, through the birth and growth and eventual departure of sons (neither of us was blessed with a daughter, who might have stuck), and we have survived the deaths of our spouses just when we might have reasonably supposed that the best years, the liberated years, were about to begin.

We didn't enjoy, as it turned out, the fruit of our long labors in the matrimonial vineyard. (My labors, it is true, were a little less conscientiously carried out than Tom's. He nursed his wife through two bouts of cancer while I could afford to hire people to help when Vincent began to die.) And yet neither one of us has been looking for a replacement in the two and three years, respectively, since those deaths. I know in my case it seemed easier simply to assume that that part of life was over. For Tom, perhaps, it was different—I don't know.

In any event, after the awful party I invited Tom to follow me home for a drink, and it amused me to notice that he is still driving the kind of car I might have settled for in my twenties— an ancient Chrysler with bulging headlights and, he assured me, the original finish and interior. I don't know anything about cars, on principle—I drive the sort of practical, small, four-wheel-drive pickup that makes sense in these mountains— but I do remember when everyone graduating from college acquired Tom's kind of car, secondhand, and used it through graduate school or the first couple of jobs. By now, though, we've all moved on to something more sedate and, inevitably, more expensive.

Owning an old car certainly didn't make Tom appear a failure in my eyes. In fact I liked his lack of pretension, which also showed in the way he dressed that evening: unpressed jeans and a pale blue button-down shirt, well-faded, also unpressed. I like my men to look self-possessed but I've never cared for dandies, and it was a relief to see that Tom wore rather scruffy sneakers. I would have liked him less, I admit, if he'd worn those heavy laced-up black shoes that make men look, from the ankles down, like minor politicians.

I'm not superficial in my judgments, no matter how that last may sound, and I'd found out by the end of our first evening that Tom measured up on all accounts. He's a "cradle Democrat," as he calls himself, with passionate convictions that fall in all the right places: he's pro-choice, of course, and anti-nuke, and sees overpopulation as the world's greatest problem (neither of us seems to feel we've contributed to it, although between us we put eight children into the world). He doesn't believe in war, no matter what the provocation, an unfashionable position these days. He taught for years at a liberal-arts college in Ohio, and he's well-read in his field, which is eighteenth-century English literature, without being in the least pedantic.

I'm a teacher, too—not retired yet, thank God, because the local school system needs me—and it's very important to me to be able to discuss books. I mean, "the other," as my mother, bless her heart, always called sex, is very important—you can't have lived through the sixties without acknowledging that—but all passion fades sometime, and then it is certainly a relief to be able to turn to talking about books. Books are a passion, too, after all; at least, they are for me.

Two weeks of spending a good deal of time together—dinners, a movie, an evening dancing—haven't brought us yet to talking about books. There are too many other topics of greater interest still to be plumbed. Our lives are composed of so many layers, so many rich and contradictory details, and since we'd both lived alone for some time, and before that with rather uncommunicative spouses, we'd developed a shorthand description of everything that matters. Now, for the first time, we could afford to drop the shorthand and get down to the real significance, because each of us was in the blessed presence of someone who knew how to listen.

After a while, life, it seems to me, can be compared to a piece of embroidery in one of those kits they used to sell in chic department stores. The pattern is already inked in, and the colored yarns are provided, and all you have to do is match the yarn to the color and begin to stitch away. That's the way I'd seen my life, and the way I'd presented it to strangers, for quite some time, but on that first evening, Tom asked me not to give him "such quick answers," and I knew right away what he meant.

I was flattered. Mostly in this world we older women are *de trop*. We have so many memories and opinions by now that we tend to overwhelm other people, like heavy-masted, many-sailed ships bearing down at a great clip on a couple of becalmed rowboats.

But Tom wanted to hear. He wanted it all. Not in the preordained needlepoint-kit colors, but in colors that were true to life—or as true to the depths of shade and sunshine as I could make them. And in telling him about my marriage and my children and my teaching—all the important details of my life, in fact—I opened up a well of sadness I hadn't been aware of until then.

No tragedies, no real heartbreak, just the inevitable sadness of the wear and tear of time, the grinding down of dreams and hopes, the final acceptance of a certain level of mediocrity and dullness in everything, even in myself.

I suppose that sadness had something to do with my responsiveness to Tom. Years ago, I believed a new man signaled a new start. I'm far past that foolishness now, but the reawakening of my decent dead body did seem to presage other more lasting changes.

Making love, for me, has always been a form of conversation. What matters most is the lover's ability to listen—the texture of his silence. And Tom's had the most beautiful texture, lightly grained, like fine grosgrain ribbon. And spools and spools of it. He never seemed to get tired, those first few weeks, of listening to me, and I suppose I talked more than I had in years.

Did he talk, too? Peering out the window at Mike, who has now stopped his machinery in order to eat a sandwich, I'm not sure. Certainly I would have urged Tom to share revelation for revelation, out of politeness; I was raised at a time when girls were taught how to please men. (It never occurred to us to ask why we should please them.) But whether he responded to my polite encouragements, I don't know—which makes me feel a little uneasy.

Did I talk too much?

I suppose I will never get over, or even regret, much, the pure ecstasy of that unburdening. The pouring out of all those hoarded details, which never meant anything to anybody, is like the dispersing of junk at a yard sale, when it becomes apparent that a good many people are eager to pay cash for what hardly seemed worth toting to the dump. The detritus is elevated by the attention it receives; I remember, once, snatching an old pastel print dress back from a woman who was about to buy it for a couple of dollars, because the terrible old dress was transformed by her desire. (I don't think I ever wore it, though. The magic disappeared fast.)

But still, did I talk too much?

My husband said that to me only once, in forty years, and that was when he was irritable with pain, toward the end, and I was trying to distract him with some chatter. "Louise, you talk too much; it's your only fault," he said, gasping over the heaves of his pain. And maybe because it was one of the last things he said to me, it struck home.

I thought, then, I'll never talk again, I'll never burden the air, or another human being's ears, and I was quiet for some time. (One of my sons even noticed. I didn't dare ask him whether he thought it was an improvement.) So by the time Tom was entangled with me on my white couch, I had a couple of years of words dammed up inside, words I hadn't even known existed, anymore than I'd noticed the presence of water in my life before my pump broke and my spigots began issuing air.

You have to miss something in order to value it, or even to notice it. I suppose that's the reason I've lost Tom.

For indeed I have lost him, after only two weeks. A mature voice tells me that might have been anticipated from the beginning; when something starts with great intensity, it tends to burn itself out quickly. But we were both so aware of the danger we were running, falling into each other like that; we discussed it earnestly. And neither of us has ever been a hit-and-run lover; we had years of married faithfulness to prove it. And yet I have lost Tom, after only two weeks.

Now Mike has bent to his task again, and the steel cable is beginning, laboriously, to reverse itself and wind up around the reel. This is accomplished with a sort of screeching as the tension and weight increase, and the old pump, jerked free of its roots, begins to rise.

I go outside to watch; the screeching is hard to bear. Mike

is standing attentively next to the reel with his gloved hand riding lightly on the laboring cable.

As I approach, I see that his grandsons have taken to squatting in the shade of the woodshed, and someone I assume is Mike's wife is sitting nearby on a stump. Pump replacement must be a family affair, and, remembering my attempts to corral my boys into various household chores, I wonder what magic Mike has used. Or perhaps coercion? It's summer, school is out, there is simply nothing else to do with these children.

Mike's chest, I notice, sprouts an array of antennalike white hairs, shooting out through the open neck of his brown shirt. He's tightly belted into his pants, which have the look of a uniform. I imagine the woman on the stump must have her hands full, washing a day's sweat out of these clothes. I remember one time I ran a load of laundry for Tom—the odd delight I felt in folding his socks, which seemed so small. I've washed and folded men's and boys' socks all my life, but I never noticed before how small they all are. My great long panty hose seem gross by comparison.

"We got yer old pump up," Mike says with pride, gesturing to a heavily rusted tube; I can hardly believe that all my watery wants have been taken care of, for years, by this meager instrument. "Here's your new one—bright and shiny," he says, pulling a metal cylinder out of a box. "I'll have you hitched up in no time."

"That's good," I say, "because I want to shower."

"Going out?" he asks, with a gleam, and the woman on the stump giggles. The two children squatting in the shade are silent.

"Yes, indeed—going out to dinner." Of course it is not true. But it seems suddenly that I will feel better if I can wash and dress as though I do indeed have somewhere to go. (In fact there's a nice salmon filet and some salad makings waiting for me in my refrigerator.)

"I'll have this thing going in an hour," Mike promises. "That give you time enough?"

"Just barely," I say, not wanting to grant him too much leeway.

"What time's your date?"

"I'm supposed to meet him at six." Then a lurch of pain slaps me, like a big cold wave tumbling me to my knees.

Mike busies himself with the new pump. "Where are you going to eat?" This is a small town, after all. Everyone wants to know.

I think of something, fast—something that won't have the wrong connotations. But I've forgotten that inexpensive, for me, is luxurious for Mike.

"Cafe Santa Fe," I say, thinking of little green umbrellas in a courtyard and geraniums in bushel baskets.

"The guy must like you," he says. "I took Rosa here there for our anniversary and it cost me an arm and a leg."

"Well, you have to order carefully—" and again that great slap of icy water. What a fool I am not to retreat to bed with smelling salts; what a fool to believe I can carry on an ordinary conversation on the very day I've lost Tom.

Because the truth of the matter is that Tom is the man I've been waiting for, the man whose possible existence resigned me to a long, long marriage and the silence that came with it and followed it, the man who, for me, is one in a million—and probably the only one in a million. It seems fruitless to try to explain why this is so, and so I won't try. After all, I've lost him.

I turn away and start to the house before another wave can slap me down. I notice that the woman on the stump is watching me. We women know how to smell out distress, no matter how carefully concealed.

Back at the house, I realize I can't go to bed, with or without smelling salts, because Mike is going to want to be paid as soon as the new pump is installed. So I do the sensible thing, under the circumstances: I make myself a cup of tea and wash my face with water poured from a bottle into a mixing bowl.

The water is tepid, and doesn't feel clean. My face, after I've washed it, doesn't feel clean either. My skin is stretched tightly across my bones, and I don't dare to look in the mirror. Abandoned women—all that power turns to ashes when the fire's put out.

But why abandoned? I ask myself as I sit down with my

current Trollope, to get through the time until Mike will need to be paid. Tom never promised anything. I never promised anything. Feelings change.

But what about the layer that exists below words—the smooth tense tactile layer that binds two people together? Tom's long pale back against my chest on the three nights we spent together. The crook of his knees, accommodating mine as I lay, curled, behind him. His murmur, that first night, "I can't get enough of you," and his arms tight around me.

Where does that layer go? Does it melt like ice cream left in the sun?

It was there. I smelled it, felt it, tasted it—the smooth dense layer that binds two people together.

Maybe he never felt it. Maybe to him I was no more substantial than the touch of one of my nice printed sheets. Maybe he mistook my shoulder for a pillow, my breath for a breeze through the open window beside the bed. Maybe for him I never really existed except in words—too many words, the words that now buzz remorsefully around my head.

"Why do you always explain so much?" an early boyfriend asked me.

It's all very well to cite intelligence, the need to communicate. The only thing that matters is that smooth layer below all the words.

Maybe my talking punctured it.

I won't blame myself. I have broken that habit. It's a habit that lay like a steel wrench across the first half of my life. No, I did nothing wrong. I was reasonable, I didn't ask for explanations, promises. But the future, in spite of my reasonableness, took on a pinkness, a glow.

It is very hot. It will always be very hot, I think, with the assurance that comes from foundering in the moment. Any moment will do. I've bogged down.

Thunder begins in the east and arcs across the sky to the west. The sheen of the clouds darkens; we are in for a storm. Perhaps that will hurry Mike along, up at the well.

Finally, around five, the first big, round drops of rain hit my deck, and at the same time, Mike is hammering on my kitchen door.

He is beaming with satisfaction. "All hooked up and ready to go."

I turn on water in the kitchen sink; the gush is rewarding. Then I thank Mike profusely and pay his not-large bill. As I write out the check, I notice how clean and purposeful my letters and numbers look. Anyone reading that check would believe I was in perfect control—a woman sitting in the middle of her life, casting out into still water, pulling up the gracious monsters of the deep.

Mike drives off, scattering gravel. I see his two grandsons' faces pasted like daisies to the rear window. The wife is a dark shape inside the truck's cab.

Now at last they are gone, and I can take my shower. I turn on the water and adjust it carefully, then get out of my clothes. As I step into the shower, I catch a glimpse of myself in the mirror: a tall, stout, middle-aged woman, her stomach and breasts looking massive with age.

I can't bear that. I turn away into the shower.

As I begin, mechanically, to shampoo my hair, I know the lack of an engagement for the evening means nothing; I am at ease and easy alone. Even the loss of companionship and the early heat of sex mean very little. What is breaking my heart is the loss of the layer under words that binds two people together.

I am standing in the shower, my first shower in two days, standing absolutely still under the gracious, streaming water— a woman still young in an old woman's body, a woman crying.

Because everything ends. I know everything ends. I know it inside my sturdy old bones.

I must begin, once more, to build my faith on that—the faith that fell apart so fast yesterday and today, because my call was not returned, my proposed plan for a weekend together not endorsed. I must build my faith grain by grain on the bone of my understanding: that all things change. That all things pass.

That even the man I spent my life waiting for has passed like a rowboat heading quietly from the harbor into the open sea.

Rat

Rat held on hard to her own life. (She called herself Rat. Other people called her Rebecca.) She knew its value because she'd tried more than once to lose it—direct attempts, and indirect: drugs, motorcycles, crazy boyfriends. Now, in late middle age, she'd learned to hold onto her life as she held onto her periwinkle-blue five-pound dumbbells: with a steady, unrelenting, two-fisted grip.

Then happiness came. She'd never expected it. It grew like a firm weed in the soil of her intention. Perhaps her light grip on her life, earlier, had failed to sustain the seedlings she now understood held happiness—or its possibility—in their frail green shoots.

Happy, she remembered all kinds of things: the smell of her mother's hand lotion—Hinds Honey and Almond Cream. (As a child, she'd thought it was Hands, Honey, and Almond Cream.) She remembered her grandmother's stories, and the old lady's silky smell—many of her memories were built around women's delicious cakelike smells.

Once her grandmother had described a pair of rats who'd found a way to drag an egg from the kitchen to the attic, where they could devour the egg in peace: one rat lay on her back, clasping the egg with her arms and legs, while the other rat dragged her upstairs by her tail.

Rat had taken her secret name from that story. She believed the greatest difference between rodents and human beings (laying aside humans' ridiculous fear of anything that scuttled) was the rodents' ability to hold on. In her grandmother's story, the rat knew exactly how to hold the egg firmly enough to carry it without fracturing its delicate shell.

RAT WORKED WITH HER FRIEND Vicky at the realty company they'd started when they first came to Santa Fe, two women with a lot of history behind them and a distaste for small Midwestern towns. Each of them had a little nest egg from a divorce or an inheritance, and they used them for down payment on an adobe office right off the plaza, and for the first year's rent on two identical apartments in what were called town houses but were really barracks for migratory birds on the south side of town.

These arrangements were all temporary and therefore acceptable; both women knew they would move on before long.

Leaf Realty (the name was their private joke) specialized in "the stem and root of the business": affordable houses, which meant three bedrooms with hot tub on a cul-de-sac on the east side for under two hundred thousand. Leaf did not represent the huge castles on the northern heights or the barracks and rabbit warrens on the south side.

The women's quickness at finding a nitch paid off. After two years, they were making good money, and they moved into an attractive condo on Artist Road, with a view of the ski basin and a nearby park for jogging.

As part of their good fortune, each of them acquired what in their new parlance they referred to as lovers. In the old days, they would have called them boyfriends.

Vicky's lover, Luiz, was a slight, mustachioed Mexican who'd come up to Santa Fe to help his mother die; she'd been employed as housekeeper at the governor's mansion, moving through administration after administration, which were all the same to her—the same duties, the same competence, were required. Now Mrs. Santero was waiting quietly for her end in the second bedroom in her son's double-wide, parked in El Paradiso Trailer Park between Santa Fe and Albuquerque.

While he waited for his mother's death, Luiz started a garden-maintenance service that was soon much in demand. He was as devoted to his swatches of moist velvety grass, his delphiniums and foxgloves, as he was to Vicky, whom, both women agreed, he adored.

Rat had found a hard-working artist (a contradiction in terms, she told Vicky) who actually put bread on his table with exquisite renderings of hollyhocks and mountain vistas. Randy was dissatisfied with this use of his extraordinary skill, but after all, they reasoned together, he was on the verge of actually beginning to save money, and then he would find what it had been, all these years, he had really meant to paint.

Rat liked Luiz—she appreciated that Vicky had crossed a line, loving a Mexican—but Vicky appeared only to tolerate Randy. She told Rat, once, that she didn't see what Randy contributed, which inspired Rat to go down the list: ample and rewarding lovemaking, a good wit, a passion for reading serious books, knowledge of all the local hiking trails. And that, Rat told Vicky, was only a bare summary; the warmth she felt when she was with Randy was perhaps self-generated, but that did not make it less delightful. She was the sun in the relationship, she realized, to his cool distant moon, but having wanted all her adult life to feel that she could love, Rat was quite satisfied; and Randy was beaming.

Rat couldn't help hoping that Randy would one day embark on a series of portraits of her daily life: gardening, cooking, laughing with Vicky as they set out in the company Land Rover to show a new client something promising. She felt—no, she knew—there were moments most painterly in her ordinariness, that it was this ordinariness, in fact, that lent a picturesque quality not found in the old days, when she was taken by a lover to Paris, or treated by a husband to a week at a spa.

"It's the grit," she told Vicky, who understood. Painting was grit laid on canvas, Rat believed, and she sensed that Randy—at least Randy before he got sick—would have agreed with her.

But where in all this was her grip on her own life, her rat's proven ability to hold the precious egg tight enough to carry it yet not fracture its fragile shell?

"It's the way I'm handling him," she explained to Vicky, who'd asked something prodding one late-fall morning when they were taking their lattée break on a bench outside the Plaza Cafeteria. Rather, this being Santa Fe, it was their tea break: warm, pallid. "I haven't changed one iota of my routine, which means I'm holding on."

"You're running home two or three times a day to look in on him," Vicky reminded her.

"Only as long as he has this fever. He won't drink enough

otherwise, even when I leave bottled water and fruit juice by the bed."

"He'd drink enough if you weren't there to hold the cup to his lips."

Rat laughed. "I don't hold the cup to his lips. I just bring up some fresh orange juice, or a lattée."

"Well, you've made your bed, as our mothers used to say," Vicky told her. "Just don't let this spoil the winter. We've got a lot coming up at the office."

"It's not going to spoil anything," Rat said.

A chill set in then between the two women, and they fell silent. Rat knew Vicky was resisting asking what was wrong with Randy. He wouldn't go to a doctor—he didn't believe in them, and besides, he had no insurance. Rat was skilled enough to nurse anyone out of colds and flu (she'd grown up in a large family, the eldest daughter in charge of all kinds of minor misfortune), but after two weeks of Randy's constant low-grade fever, she had become alarmed. She'd asked him to move into her condo, temporarily, of course, because she didn't feel he should be alone at night.

"He groans in his sleep," she told Vicky.

"I know. I've heard him."

A cloud passed over the sterling sun. The plaza was draped in shadows and the temperature dropped precipitously. Both women clutched their coats and stood up.

"I'm worried sick," Rat said. "You remember when Luiz broke his arm falling out of that tree, and we took him in for a while–"

"He wouldn't use the painkillers, none of us slept for a week–"

"It's like that. We help when we're needed," Rat said, wondering how that would look on one of their ads.

"I know," Vicky said, patting her arm. "I just hate to see you so exhausted."

"I can't just turn him out. He doesn't know how to take care of himself, and he has no family, except for a sister in Grand Rapids," Rat said, remembering Randy's description of his gradual desertion by his quarreling family. "They don't believe in artists."

COMING INTO HER BEDROOM that evening, Rat stood still for a moment, watching Randy's sleeping face. With his knees drawn to his chest, he looked like a folded bird but also like an explorer facing death on an ice floe. Rat spread the extra blanket over his feet.

He stirred and opened his eyes. "Home early?"

"My regular time. It's just after five. Think you could eat something?" She sat on the side of the bed and stroked his thin, light hair. She could feel his fever like a pulse entering her fingers.

"Maybe some soup," he said. She'd had success earlier in the week with her homemade chicken broth.

"I don't have any more soup, except out of a can," she said.

He sighed. "All right. Could you rub my feet?"

Rat turned back the covers. His long, pale feet lay huddled together; she took one in the palm of her hand. Rubbing his gnarled toes, she wondered at their whiteness. They looked like tubers, long hidden from the sun. And they were very cold. After a while, she buried them again under the covers and went down to the kitchen.

She opened a can of broth and heated it, adding a sprig of parsley for color.

When she carried the soup up, Randy was asleep; she left the tray beside the bed and went down to read the newspaper.

She slept poorly that night, next to the furnace that was Randy's capsized body. Waking at an unearthly hour, she remembered how he'd pounded on their front door, that first evening, how he'd hurried to her with a big bouquet of flowers. Was it being loved that undid men?

Lying next to him, she began to say her prayers, hoping to find a few hours' sleep before the alarm. Her prayers usually held the seed of sleep, but this time they were void. Her whole life was hollowing out, to make way for something invasive, substantial.

Early next morning, Rat sat at the kitchen table with her

coffee and the big family medical encyclopedia. She looked up *Fever*, and *Exhaustion* (the long entry called it *Prostration*–the encyclopedia was fifteen years old), *Depression*, and his newest symptom, *Difficulty with Urination*. Now Randy sat desolately on the toilet for long periods, without success, which he blamed on the effects of aging. But the medical encyclopedia offered another cause.

Rat closed the encyclopedia carefully, as though the sound might wake him. Her father had died of lung cancer, and she'd watched her mother's life pale in the intensity of that illness' glare. Once, late at night after speechless hours of pain and support–the pillow freshened, the water glass refilled, the hand tender on the tossing head–her mother had said, "I tried to get him to stop smoking years ago."

Rat dressed for her day at work, laying her cosmetic brushes down next to the basin with great care, opening the closet door slowly so it wouldn't creak. Finally she crept downstairs in her stocking feet and let herself out into the fresh cool air. There was snow on the northern mountains.

At lunchtime, she made several calls to doctor friends and a nurse she'd known for years; their answers to her questions, while contingent on many factors ("You really ought to get him in here for tests," one of the doctors said), confirmed her fears. Perhaps, she thought as she hung up from the last call, that was what she wanted: a confirmation of the worst possible outcome.

That evening she made Randy another big pot of chicken soup, and took him a large bowl. "I'm staying here till you eat it all," she told him, smiling.

As he slowly spooned up the soup, she asked him, again, to go to a doctor, and left a name and phone number printed large on the pad beside the bed.

"I won't make the appointment for you," she said, feeling that this was the first of an important set of distinctions. "But I'll take time off from work and drive you whenever you need to go."

Randy glanced at the name and number and set the soup bowl down. "That was good," he said. "I ate it all."

That night he took her in his arms, but as had been true for weeks now, there was nothing more he could do. Rat tried her humble best to help him, and he was grateful and told her so, but later she heard the deeply-drawn, dry breathing of his despair.

Randy didn't make an appointment to see the doctor. Rat hardly expected him to. What would be the use, she wondered now, of his hearing what they both already knew?

"He's very sick," she told Vicky when they were jogging around the track in the park below their condos. Vicky didn't ask what was wrong. Instead, she said, with her runner's even breath, "You're going to nurse him through it?"

"I don't know yet," Rat said. Ahead of them, a panel truck

was parked, and the driver leaned out to call to them. Vicky and Rat smiled; they were past the time when they would have labeled such attention annoying.

"It may be a long haul," Vicky said.

"I know." Rat wondered if on the other side she would still be young enough to attract attention.

As they rounded the last curve, she said, "If I leave him now, he's still well enough to get up and make an effort to find another woman, one who would stick. Later he won't be able to."

Vicky said, "You're being realistic."

"I have to hold on to my own life."

"I support you there," Vicky said. "Remember when Luiz wanted to hike one of those mountains in Colorado, and I told him it was too late in the fall to risk it?"

The comparison seemed trivial, but Rat nodded.

"He couldn't have gotten me out if there was a blizzard, and I wasn't sure I could get out on my own."

"Or help him."

"That, too." Vicky opened the sports-complex door. "Let's shower. Be careful what you're getting into, Rebecca."

The name sounded foreign to Rat.

She arrived home at five that evening and started pasta sauce. When it was ready—the onions, tomatoes, and green peppers melded into a satisfactory, garlic-rich mass—she called to Randy. She heard his bare feet hit the floor. When he came down in her old bathrobe and his sneakers, the laces flapping, she saw how much weight he had lost.

He sat at the kitchen table, supporting his head with his hand, and obediently spooned in the pasta. But after a few mouthfuls, he excused himself, and Rat heard him retching in the bathroom.

She went in and wiped his face with a wet towel.

"I'm sorry," he gasped. The bathroom reeked sourly. "All the trouble I'm causing you."

"I chose it," Rat said. She'd wondered about that, before. Now she knew she had chosen it, at some moment in the dead of night when, waking, she'd felt him curled against her back. She would have to choose it, now, every day.

Her mother's saying came back to her—how she'd hated those expressions, growing up: "If you have faith as small as a mustard seed...." But what had been the end of the phrase? Rat couldn't remember.

Now she knew it was only a matter of time before Randy would agree to go to the doctor. In the thing's grip, he would thrash and struggle; but he would do whatever the doctor advised, to keep a little hope.

November brought early snow; at sunset, the mountains burned red, and Rat remembered why the conquistadors had called them "Sangre de Cristo." She began to improve her self-care, starting a new course of vitamins, watching her diet, eliminating coffee. At night Randy sometimes held her in his arms.

At the end of the month, she saw the pad with the doctor's name and number lying on the bed by his knee.

Next day, the pad was back on the bedside table.

"I'm going to have to decide soon," she told Vicky the following morning.

"Watch out for yourself," Vicky said, and for a moment Rat thought she'd called her by her secret name.

Vicky was planning to take Luiz to Hawaii for Thanksgiving; she told Rat she didn't mind paying for the trip, since Luiz would give her a good time. "Quid pro quo," she joked.

Rat was not making plans for Thanksgiving. She didn't know how to regenerate the old habits, the old systems. The large, invasive thing had moved in.

"I'm going to spend Thanksgiving absolutely quietly," she told Randy. He looked surprised; in their first months together, Rat had always been planning an outing or a get-together, a potluck, a hike, or a dinner party. "Is there something you want to do?" she asked, surprised.

"My sister called this morning," Randy said. "She's visiting in Taos. If you don't mind, I think I'll go up there for Thanksgiving. I haven't seen her in a long time, and I really enjoy my niece. Mindy," he said, as though testing the name.

"Sounds like a great idea. You won't mind if I don't go along?"

"You need the rest," Randy said generously.

It was extraordinary to see him get up, shave, shower, and dress on Thanksgiving morning; extraordinary to see him bring his good suit out of the closet and examine it carefully for stains; extraordinary to see him polish his shoes, find his wallet and keys, slide into his parka. "I'll be back before dark," he promised, kissing her cheek. Rat knew his sister would notice how he had changed, but Randy, exuberant, freed, reignited, would be able to persuade her it meant nothing—a bout of flu, working too hard, exercising too much. His sister might not be hard to reassure.

Rat spent the day combing through her mother's old prayer book for the mustard seed quote; she felt sure it was in one of the parables. As daylight faded, she looked up at the blood-colored mountains. Randy would drive through them on his way home.

She found the quote as the sun was setting. It was not exactly the way she remembered it—it hardly could have been:

"For verily I say unto you, if ye have faith as a grain of mustard seed, ye shall say unto this mountain, Remove hence to yonder place, and it shall remove; and nothing shall be impossible unto you."

But the thing was not a mountain. It had tentacles, it could pierce.

Randy came in a little later, flushed and fresh-smelling, the wintry air in his skin and hair. Rat kissed him hungrily; he was excited, he seemed young.

"My niece and her best friend, Lucy, are planning to go to Paris for Christmas," he told her. "Their first time. They've asked me to go along. You wouldn't mind–?"

"Vicky and I always have to be here for the holidays, it's one of our busiest times," Rat said, feeling relieved and sore.

"My sister won't rest easy if the girls go over alone, and it'll give you a rest from all this care." For a moment, they both believed the care was over, finished, no longer needed, that love could bloom for them, still, and long life.

"Sounds like a good idea all around," Rat said. "When you come home, you can move back to your own place."

"You plan on it," he said, stripping off his parka. "And we'll start having fun again."

Rat took a breath. "No," she said. "You may start having fun again, but not with me." She was imagining the niece's friend, a pretty blond with a sense of adventure. How grateful Rat was at the thought of her youth, her enthusiasm.

"You're tired," Randy said, kissing her. "A break is what we both need. It'll be different, when I get back."

But Randy did not make the trip to Paris. By then he'd visited the doctor; by then Rat had helped him move to Taos where his sister and his niece would take over his care. The

Paris trip was put off until Easter, when, Randy told Rat over the telephone, he expected to be well enough to go. He was not bitter, or hurt, or angry; he was concentrating all his energy on getting well, and negative thoughts about Rat or anyone else, he said, could block that process. He was scheduled to undergo an operation in late January.

After that, Rat heard, periodically, from his sister, who felt an obligation to keep her informed. "After all," Louise said during one of their weekly telephone calls, "you took care of him for the first three months."

"And you are taking care of him for the last three."

"That's what it looks like." Louise sighed. "Mindy's helping, and Lucy drops in now and then. That really cheers him up."

Rat realized then she'd waited a little too long. Her softness of heart had limited Randy's choices. Still, she had the consolation of knowing that, to the end, he lifted his head and smiled when Lucy came in the room. And to the end they talked of going to Paris, in the spring.

The Hunt

Heidi was charmed by the courtship. Not one of the many men she'd known, including her long-ago husband, had gone to the head of the family to ask for her hand, or even been able to imagine such a term. And although it pained her to laughter to admit even this one time that her older brother Harold was now as he had always desired to be, the head of that amorphous tangle even Heidi acknowledged as family, she was deeply touched by what had happened. The ancient form, adhered to in all its outdated quaintness, seemed to set her at a very high price.

Of course Larry had not been asking to marry her. No one married, these days, except the very young. He had been imagining, and outlining (so Heidi believed) a long-term relationship, something with little of whim or impulse in it. Harold's understanding and eventual acceptance was needed because, as Larry reminded Heidi, who grimaced, she would not be happy with a man her brother found unsatisfactory. Larry perhaps had been too tactful to mention—or perhaps, being Larry, he'd never thought of it—that Heidi was dependent on her brother's generosity to keep her little house in Santa Fe and her relatively carefree life.

When she was disgusted with that life, which did not give her much to chew on, as she sometimes said, since she was retired from city government and not interested in volunteer work or aimless socializing, Heidi liked to imagine that primordial scene between Harold and Larry.

It had taken place on a Saturday morning, six months earlier; Harold generally spent Saturdays going over his stamp collection or attending to his assortment of firearms. So Larry would have found him occupied, perhaps down on his knees in his library with cans and rags and newspapers spread out and the gun cabinet standing open and half-empty behind him. But even that task, which he adored, would not have prevented Harold from looking up at his visitor and understanding, at once, that serious attention was needed.

Harold would then have stood up—with ease, for a

seventy-year-old—dusting off his knees and offering the man he'd been calling "Heidi's beau" a softly-upholstered armchair.

From that point, Heidi, even at her most animated, could not imagine the scene. Harold might have sat in his desk chair, although he would certainly have pulled it out, first, from behind the mahogany partner's desk that had been their father's; Harold did not depend on gestures and positions to communicate his authority, which had been his like a birthright, Heidi thought, since he was seven years old and claimed all the stars in heaven on a summer night, as well as the moon.

"You can have the evening star," he'd told a tearful Heidi, who had already understood, at three, that her brother took what he claimed. There may even have been a time or two, she knew, over the many years since, when she had been grateful to be allowed to have the evening star.

But what the two men, so different, and cast in such different roles in terms of Heidi, could have actually said, she was not able to imagine. Larry had been reticent on the subject, merely saying that the talk had gone well and that Harold had seemed to understand. But what the texture, and the details, of that talk and that putative understanding had been, Heidi realized she might never know.

Now—six months after the conversation—Heidi and Larry were going to spend their first weekend with Harold and

Laura, a cold weekend in November; the aspens had lost their leaves and the piñon nuts had fallen and been gathered. Harold and Laura lived twenty miles southeast of Santa Fe in the family house where Heidi had spent summers in childhood; as soon as he was released from his Michigan university, at retirement age, with a good pension and many honors, Harold had packed up a slightly-protesting Laura and driven out to Pecos to reopen the house and occupy it year-round.

According to the terms of their father's will, the house was to be for Harold's sole use, and he was responsible for its considerable expenses. However, Heidi knew her father had intimated that she should be invited to share the old place as often as possible; and for five years, Harold had honored that agreement scrupulously, inviting his sister to Thanksgiving and Christmas and to all large parties. But she had never before been asked to spend the night. Nor had Larry been included.

That in itself was significant, Heidi thought as she sat beside Larry in the front seat of her Jeep. Larry was driving with his usual concentration and thoroughness, as though nothing else could be happening in the world—which was the reason he considered the radio an annoying distraction. As they rode along the throughway in the humming silence, Heidi told Larry she felt they were being invited to spend two nights—not one, but two—because of the way he had approached Harold to ask him for his permission. Heidi felt full of generosity when she made such concessions.

"I wasn't exactly asking for permission," Larry said with his journalist's exactitude, which annoyed and delighted Heidi about equally. "I just wanted to give him a chance to tell me what he thought."

This was a new view of the situation, and not a very satisfactory one. "I guess if he'd expressed some reservation, you'd have just given me up," Heidi said.

"Maybe for the time being. I know how important Harold and Laura are to you. But I'd have asked him again," Larry said.

That felt a little better. It was one thing, Heidi thought, to hang in the balance—she had been hanging in one balance or another her entire life—and another to feel her brother's hand on the scale. "I should hope you wanted me enough to try again," she said. Already, she seemed to be a habit of Larry's, along with not eating meat, volunteering at the animal shelter, and protesting, gently enough, to women he met wearing fur coats. To Heidi, habits were prunelike facts, shriveled and hard, with very little juice left after the long drying of practice.

Larry answered something automatic, then saw her disappointment and tried to improve on what he'd said—or what he hadn't said. Meanwhile Heidi concentrated on the pale blue sky unfolding over the mountains; the early-morning clouds were clearing and a honey-colored sun looked out. "Maybe the dripping will have stopped by this afternoon," she said, remembering the fringe of ragged pines around the old house. It had always held fog and damp and rain and dew long after the surrounding fields were dry.

They turned in at the green gate, which hadn't been repainted in Heidi's memory, passed the big mailbox on its stick, bent almost to the breaking point years earlier by a reckless mailman, and proceeded down the sandy rut that could hardly be called a drive. Part of the reason the house was kept in a state of permanent decrepitude was that Harold had always feared being labeled ostentatious; he had spent his life grubbing (as Heidi thought of it) in the literature department of a mediocre state university when he might have retired early and cultivated all kinds of pleasant habits.

Even Laura, his wife of so many years—Heidi was astonished when she thought of the sum—had spent most of her forties and fifties, after their five children were grown, laboring away at the city hospital, passing out books and holding hands; the couple had seemed, during those decades, so hard-pressed and so benevolent that Heidi had shrunk from the comparison. All those years she'd traveled, painted a little, tried modern dance, taken up all kinds of habits and hobbies and nurtured or dropped them; the song of her freedom seemed a reproach to the dull drone of her brother's responsibleness, not to speak of

Laura's, who had always seemed an admirable but pathetic martyr to Harold's way of life (including, Heidi would have liked to intimate, five children and now all kinds of grandchildren with their escalating demands).

Heidi, all those years after her divorce, had stayed single, sampling men cautiously but with a kind of ease she knew she'd have lost, once and for all, if she'd married or had children or pursued some solemn career.

Larry parked her Jeep under one of the dripping pines and sat for a moment, studying the house's long brown facade. "Such a big place for two people."

"In the old days, in the summertime, when our parents and their generation were alive, every bedroom had at least one body in it." Heidi reached for the door handle. "Get my suitcase, would you?"

Then she stood waiting while Larry took out their two suitcases, or rather, hers, and his backpack. Heidi had given up suggesting that he join the adult world and buy himself a wallet, a suitcase, and some leather shoes; he had principles that prevented such compromises, and Heidi was well on her way, laboriously, to appreciating his honesty.

She walked up the broken brick path ahead of him and saw the outline of Laura's head inside the screen door. As her sister-in-law opened it, Heidi stepped forward with a spurt of her old enthusiasm and kissed Laura.

Heidi didn't introduce Larry; of course Laura knew him—at least, she had met him several times. Still, it was an omission, for Heidi, of a grace note she valued because she felt such efforts smoothed the path for Larry, who had no family of his own and sometimes seemed almost in awe of hers.

That was an uncomfortable notion, which Heidi dismissed at once. She did not want her lover to be in awe of anything or anyone. If he cherished a bit of reverence for her, that was more than sufficient, especially in the heat of their intimacy. Stepping into the dark porch, Heidi remembered the embroidered lingerie-covers her mother had used on trips to cover her stockings and girdle when they were left, briefly, on a hotel bedroom chair. "Your father shouldn't be exposed to that sort of thing," she'd said.

Laura and Larry were chatting behind her, and Heidi admired her lover's easy way.

At the end of the long hall with its jammed bookcases and mounted heads of elk and moose, Harold was waiting, his finger in a book. His tall frame was propped against the doorpost as though, Heidi thought, he was posing for his portrait, one of those moody brown-and-tan full-length oils their father might have commissioned, years ago. *Boy with Book*, something like that.

As she kissed him, however, Heidi realized that something had changed in her brother's skin. His cheek was as dry as the heel of a loaf.

She looked up at him inquiringly. Harold's pale blue eyes seemed to be examining her from a distance, as once he had examined his extensive collection of butterflies. "Are you all right?" Heidi asked, and managed to include Laura in the question.

"Just getting old," Harold said, and turned to shake hands, heartily, with Larry.

Heidi was perplexed. Although she was only four years younger than her brother, and exactly the same age as Laura, she had never felt old, or even thought much about it. When occasionally the clerk in the grocery asked if she qualified for a discount, she laughed as though such a question was preposterous, and, once in her car, quickly applied more lipstick. "Age is such a tricky thing," Heidi would sometimes say, or "It's all in the eye of the beholder."

Yet her brother's cheek felt old. And Laura, if she was not sick, looked old—faded and shrunken. Something had changed with the change in the weather; when they were last together, it had been Indian summer, and they'd sat out on the lawn—all three—shelling peas and telling stories. At a time like that, the distance that separated Heidi and Harold from their shared, contentious childhood had seemed so slight Heidi could have bridged it with her little finger.

"Moth is here," Laura confided as she led Heidi to her old bedroom down the hall. "We didn't expect her, she just showed up."

Heidi was instantly alert. "Trouble?"

"Robert says she won't go back to school."

"Well, Robert and Tiny encouraged her all those years to do just exactly what she wanted to do," Heidi said, taking her suitcase from Laura and dumping it on the narrow, lumpy cot. "I guess this is the outcome anyone could have predicted. Remember when she threw fits over going to nursery school and Robert and Tiny took her out?"

"Moth was awfully young and shy," Laura murmured, protecting her youngest son and his wife from criticism. She stood with arms akimbo as Heidi unsnapped the locks on the suitcase. When Heidi threw back the lid, a faint scent of roses filled the room, and the bright-colored clothes in the suitcase seemed to levitate.

"Let me help you," Laura said as Heidi began to take out her clothes, and with an impulsive gesture that felt like generosity and caring, Heidi thrust a bunch of orange-and-yellow lingerie into Laura's hands.

"You have such pretty things," Laura said as she folded the lingerie and laid it in a drawer. Heidi would have liked to hear a note of sadness, of jealousy, even—Laura wore the kind of white cotton underpants that are sold in packs of three—but she failed to detect more than the slight curiosity of a relative who already knows all she needs to know.

"Are you supposed to persuade Moth to go back to school?"

Heidi asked as she lined up her cosmetics on the frayed bureau scarf. The mirror was tarnished, and as she peered at her reflection, she might also have been seeing the ten-year-old who hoarded her first lipsticks on that same scrap of linen.

"Oh, I'm out of it," Laura told her with relief. "Harold is going to handle it."

"How?"

Laura smiled, turning from the bureau. "I don't really know. You can ask him," she added, as though conferring an honor.

But in fact there was no opportunity, for Moth was with them from the next moment on.

She was a pretty seventeen-year-old, Heidi decided after watching her sitting motionless and silent at the dinner table, not eating a thing. Her dyed blond hair was cut very short, with ragged points over her temples, and her square child's hands, when she laid them on the table, were decorated with bright blue nail polish. The jeans and tight T-shirt she wore might as well have been a uniform, and even her air of dismay and scorn was familiar from countless videos and advertisements. She'd been formed, Heidi guessed, more by the currents she swam in than by her parents, conscientious Robert and his hard-working spouse, the oddly-misnamed Tiny. Moth was their only child, and Heidi remembered protesting when she heard they were going to give the baby that name. This outcome might have been expected, even then.

Larry, to his credit, was laboring to make conversation with Moth, who was seated on his left. His newspaper had recently inaugurated a young people's corner, or page—Heidi couldn't remember which—and Larry was soliciting Moth's reaction to its contents. Predictably, she hadn't read it, or anything else in the past year, Heidi guessed, and she answered his inquiries with a pouting grimace, as though to say, What fool is this that thinks I could possibly be interested—?

Laura came to the rescue, offering Moth something else to eat since the roast lamb didn't seem to be to her liking. The girl brightened up at once and soon devoured the bowl of spaghetti Laura produced—spaghetti absolutely plain, as Moth had decreed, which was the only way she could eat it.

Heidi expected Larry to ask for some spaghetti, too, then saw with astonishment that he was already eating his lamb.

The rest of them were also enjoying the lamb, which Laura said she'd been marinating for days. Heidi glanced at her brother, wondering if he remembered the great quarrel that had erupted, four or five years before, when she'd asked why Laura was forced to spend so much time in the kitchen. After all, it would have been perfectly possible, and appropriate, for Harold to hire a cook. She remembered with some pleasure that her brother had nearly snarled at her—"We like to do our own work"—and that Laura, with a piteous look, had asked her to change the subject.

But, truly, if it was not ill-health that made Laura look so diminished, it was certainly, Heidi thought, forty years of servitude. Harold never asked for it, perhaps never even expected it; service was simply what his authority inspired.

Heidi wondered, as she had so often before, where the root of his authority lay. Harold was not particularly handsome or physically impressive, and age was wizening him, but even so, he had instead of the appearance of a retired professor the air of an aged magician. Harold had little humor or imagination which meant, in Heidi's estimation, that he had no great intelligence, yet now, when he looked at Moth, she instantly straightened in her chair and returned his gaze. There was not a child or an animal or a woman who could resist Harold's glance, Heidi thought, Harold's call to instant attention. He had it from their father as a gift—unearned, she felt.

She glanced at Larry, sitting across the table, and saw that his gaze was fixed on Harold's face, a half-smile lingering around his lips as though in anticipation of a particularly delicious bon mot. When he saw that Harold was bending his attention on Moth, Larry dropped his smile and began listening seriously. It was as though, Heidi thought, Larry believed Harold would want to know his impressions, later—over brandy and cigars. In that house, even brandy and cigars were possible, along with a separate time, after dinner, for the men.

As Harold continued to prod answers out of Moth about

her school (although "prod" was scarcely the word for his delicate thumbing), Heidi remembered the horror of those dinners when her parents were still alive: the stilted conversation on approved topics, directed by her father; the dead vegetables; and her mother's anxious molelike face, which seemed to quiver with apprehension around the nose— culminating in a dismal retreat by the women to her mother's bedroom, where they sat around on the bed and smoked ciga- rettes. When finally Heidi's mother would announce that they could go back to the living room, they would troop down like a herd of depressed sheep, hearing, on the way, the men's loud voices and laughter as they lingered in the dining room.

Now Laura was serving baked apples with, as a concession to decadence, a small pitcher of heavy cream.

When they had finished eating, Harold stood up and beckoned to Larry, who started away from the table, dropping his napkin. Laura bent down and picked it up. "We're going to the library," Harold said over his shoulder as they walked to the door. The three women in the dining room sat silently glancing around, as though they had found themselves deposited in a foreign railroad station.

Then Laura said, "If we all pitch in, we can have this cleaned up in half an hour."

Moth and Heidi followed her to the kitchen.

A little later, up to her elbows in soapy water (they did not

believe in dishwashers, for a reason Heidi couldn't remember),
Laura asked, "How are things going with Larry?"

"Pretty well," Heidi equivocated, glancing at Moth, who
was strangling a wineglass in a tea towel.

"You two fucking?" the girl asked.

"My goodness, Moth," Laura demurred.

But Heidi was not taken aback. "Of course," she said. This
was just the sort of question she would expect from a girl like
Moth.

"You getting married?"

Again, Laura murmured a reproach.

"I don't believe so," Heidi said, and heard with incredulity
something that sounded almost like a whine. "I never wanted
to get married, not even the first time."

But Moth was not satisfied. She set down the wineglass
with a clang on the counter and grabbed a fork, which she
wrapped in the tea towel as though savagely swaddling a baby.
"So what are you going to do? Live together, or what?"

"We don't want to live together," Heidi said circumspectly,
although she had never discussed the issue with Larry.

"Hush now, Moth—that's enough," Laura said, tipping cold
coffee out of the cups.

"How am I supposed to learn?" Moth asked reasonably.
"Or do you just want me to repeat all your mistakes?"

"What mistakes?" Heidi asked before Laura could stop her.

"Living with people you don't like," Moth said judiciously, filing the fork in a drawer. "I don't think it matters whether you're married or not. Either way, it just goes on and on."

"Young lady!" Laura exclaimed. "Whatever got into your head to imagine—"

"I have eyes, don't I?" Moth asked. "Ears, too. I heard you and Grandpa Harold arguing last night."

"We were having a serious discussion."

"You were crying," Moth said. "Remember? I saw you afterward, in the hall."

"I expect the men are ready," Laura said hastily, leading the way back to the living room.

In fact Larry and Harold didn't emerge from the library for another half hour, and when they did, they were laughing. Harold had flung his arm over the younger man's shoulders. "Larry's going with me tomorrow," he announced. "We'll have to get started at six. Coffee at five-thirty," he told Laura.

"Where are you going?" Heidi asked.

"At the last minute, Gus called to say he can't go hunting— his wife's down with a bug, and they have grandchildren on their hands—so Larry said he'd fill in," Harold explained, going to the fireplace where he began to adjust the logs. "Get me the matches, Moth. They're in the kitchen. First fire of the season!"

Moth hurried out of the room. Laura, sighing, sat down under a reading lamp and began to fish around in her basket of mending. "I hope it won't rain all day tomorrow the way it did today."

Heidi was staring at Larry, or rather, at Larry's back. He was kneeling at the fireplace, crushing up handfuls of newspaper. Harold directed him where to put them, pointing to gaps in the structure of the logs.

Then Moth came back with the matches, and Harold let her light the fire. It blazed up quickly, bathing the dark room in light. "Good dry piñon," Harold said. "Cured all summer in the woodshed."

Heidi was still looking at Larry's back. Finally he stood up and turned around. She saw the same waiting half-smile on his face she'd seen at dinner. "I'm afraid I don't have the right gear," he told Harold.

"We'll fix you up," Harold said. "Early to bed, though. We need to be off before light to get up the mountain in time."

A few minutes later, after a round of good nights, Heidi followed Larry down the long hall to her bedroom. Once inside the door, she closed it firmly and stood with her back to the knob, studying him. With careful casualness, Larry sat on the edge of the cot and began to unlace his sneakers.

"I can't believe you agreed to go," Heidi said.

He glanced up at her. "Harold doesn't want to go alone, and the other guy dropped out. I couldn't very well refuse."

Heidi felt the doorknob in her back. She pressed against it

as she said, "You told me you'd never in your life kill a living thing."

"That's right," Larry said, "but there's no chance I'm actually going to hit anything. I'll just keep Harold company."

"The first time I spent the night with you, your cat dragged in that dead squirrel and you spent almost an hour shaking the ants out before you'd bury it, so the ants wouldn't be buried alive."

"I do the best I can," Larry said, "to stick to what I believe, but sometimes circumstances—"

"Circumstances, hell," Heidi said, leaning into the doorknob. "It's not circumstances, it's Harold."

"He's my host." Larry stood up and unfastened his belt. "Now how about we drop this and go to bed."

"It's not a bed, it's a cot," Heidi said.

Half an hour later, on the floor, he had unlocked her hands and her jaws and her knees, and she was hearing the cries of her enjoyment.

Then he bit her shoulder, and she cried out sharply.

In the morning, Larry was up and dressed and gone before Heidi opened her eyes.

Laura had breakfast ready in the warm kitchen—a basket of scones, jams, and butter. The plates from the men's breakfast were already scraped and soaking in the sink.

Laura offered her the scones. "I'll just take some tea," Heidi said. She was unwilling to swallow anything solid, as though, like the pomegranate seeds, crumbs would seal her imprisonment in that house. "When will they come back?"

"Harold promised Moth he'd take her out with the shotgun late this afternoon," Laura said. She was sitting across the table, peeling potatoes, the skins spiraling over her thin hands. "That means they'll be back by five, I expect."

"Moth wants to learn how to shoot a gun?"

"You're damn right," Moth said, coming into the kitchen. She was wearing a pair of cutoffs and an inadequate T-shirt.

"Maybe you ought to concentrate on graduating from high school first," Heidi said.

Laura interposed, "Oh, Moth's going back home tomorrow, to get ready for school. It's all agreed."

"Why in the world?" Heidi stared at the girl, who had at last surprised her.

"Grandpa Harold's going to buy me a Thunderbird," Moth said. "The day after graduation. Any color I want." Seizing her advantage, she went on, "He was up in arms about the noise you made last night."

Heidi glared at the girl. "What in the world are you talking about?"

"Caterwauling like an alley cat in heat," Moth said. Then, sensing from the two women's faces that she had gone too far, she added, "That's just what Grandpa said, at breakfast. I didn't hear a thing. But then, my room's at the other end of the house."

Heidi was dumbfounded. Something like shame began to creep into her eyes, shrouding them with tears.

"Just ignore her," Laura said, reaching across the table to pat her hand.

Heidi snatched her hand away. "It's all very well for you to put up with everything—"

"Moth, go put the laundry in the dryer, I just heard the washer stop," Laura said.

Moth sauntered toward the door to the laundry room.

"Ears in the back of her head," Laura said with pale humor. "Now, what's going on with you, Heidi?"

"You put up, and put up," Heidi astonished herself by saying. "I've watched you for years. You let Harold tyrannize you."

"I don't call it tyranny," Laura said, picking up the next potato.

"You gave up a promising career...."

"I didn't have the talent to be a professional dancer. My goodness, Heidi, that was so long ago!"

"But you were so alive then! I saw you! Dancing what was it, Stravinsky, at the armory?"

"It was 'Singing in the Rain,'" Laura corrected mildly.

"Whatever! You were alive, then...."

Moth came quietly back into the room and sat down at the table. "Can I listen, Grandma Laura?"

"No!" Heidi said.

"If you cross your heart and hope to die you won't repeat anything you hear," Laura answered.

The girl crossed her heart. "I just want to learn," she told Heidi. "I mean, the four of you are so fucked up–"

"That's enough," Laura interrupted, "or I'll send you to your room. Heidi and I are having a serious conversation."

The girl nodded.

"You've been a martyr all your life," Heidi told Laura. "You let my brother make all the decisions, enslave you for his comfort. He couldn't begin to live this way"–and she gestured at the warm kitchen, all its appliances lined up and waiting–"if he didn't have your free labor. You know it's not fair! He's never done a thing for you! He doesn't even listen to you!"

"But I love him," Laura said. "I like doing things for him. I always have. Didn't you notice how much he enjoyed my roast lamb last night?"

"Oh, I give up, I just give up," Heidi said, pushing her chair back from the table. "You are never going to change."

"Are you?" Laura asked.

Already halfway turned to the door, Heidi turned back. "I'm changing all the time!"

Moth looked at her fixedly, then turned her gaze back to Laura.

"I don't see any evidence of it," Laura said, getting up to

throw the potato skins into the garbage. Then she dropped the peeled potatoes in the sink and began to run water over them. "Remember, I've know you more than thirty years. And I've watched you do the same thing, time after time—oh, Harold and I have talked a lot about it. That's why he was so glad to see you'd finally found a decent man."

"So that's why he gave his permission. I wondered exactly what quality—"

"His permission, as you call it, is conditional."

"Conditional on what?"

"On your seeming happy and well-taken-care-of. And you do seem happy—we've all noticed it."

"Of all the damned gall—"

"What's gall?" asked Moth.

"And now you're going to wreck this relationship, too." Laura turned from the sink and stood leaning against it, her arms folded. "I could tell last night you were ready to skin that poor guy."

Moth laughed, then covered her mouth.

"Larry's a pacifist," Heidi said. "He's been that way all his life. He was planning to go to Canada during Vietnam but then the war ended. He never has eaten meat that I know of till that damned lamb, last night." For an instant, it seemed that had been the whole problem—the mouthful of meat Larry had politely swallowed. "He could have asked for spaghetti, like Moth—"

"It wasn't all that great," the girl said.

"But no. He had to do what he thought Harold wanted him to do. And now this." Heidi clenched her fists.

"Just walking on the mountain with a shotgun," Laura reminded her. "Larry's never handled a gun in his life, he won't be able to shoot an elk. Just keeping Harold company."

"It's the principle," Heidi said. "How can I respect him if he sacrifices an important principle? Just to keep Harold happy?"

"I guess he likes him," Moth said judiciously. "Last night at dinner he couldn't keep his eyes off him."

"That's enough, Moth," Laura said, and she stepped toward Heidi as though to embrace her. Heidi moved quickly out of the way. "At least give this one a chance, Heidi. Remember that poor guy at the university–the one you kicked out in the street because you said he had a 'drinking problem.' A couple of beers was all I ever saw–"

"Passed out in front of the television at seven every evening!"

Laura went on quickly. "And that Mike–he took you abroad, bought you that gold and diamond necklace–"

"Wow," Moth said.

"I never wore it, I didn't even want it!"

"Then you drove him away because he had children he needed to visit every other weekend."

"He was enmeshed!"

"And on and on," Laura said gently, reaching out to touch Heidi's shoulder. "And on and on and on. None of us is that young anymore, Heidi. You need to think about your future. It can be pretty lonely, getting old by yourself."

"I can't love a man I don't respect," Heidi said.

That ended the conversation. The afternoon passed in fits of rain and long periods of silence. The three women avoided each other, smiling when they passed in the hall or met in the kitchen. Eventually Moth retreated to the television in the library, and Laura announced she was going to take a nap. Heidi knew how rare that was—once, she had asked Laura if she might have chronic fatigue.

Around five o'clock Heidi took her book to the window seat in the living room. Rain streamed down the panes, which felt cold to her fingers. She found herself tracing the path of the drops, her book open on her knee. Somewhere, a clock struck, and the light began to fail. Laura passed on her way to the kitchen to start dinner.

Then the old wooden-sided station wagon hove into the drive. It swayed and crashed through deep puddles, its windshield wipers sawing. From the front hall window, Heidi could just see the faces of the two men, behind the wipers.

On top of the station wagon, a dark bulk was roped. When the car pulled up, Heidi saw the white antlers.

She ran to the front door. "Who shot it?" she shouted across the wet yard, where the men were slowly approaching. "Who shot the elk?"

Harold was grinning, his thin hair pinned to his head with wet, his slicker streaming. "Would you believe it, this tenderfoot here—"

Heidi turned and ran to her bedroom. She lay down on the cot and buried her face in the pillow.

Larry came in and began silently to take off his wet clothes.

Heidi looked around at him. "The uniform of forgotten armies," she said as he piled the wet fatigues on her chair. "I never thought the day would come."

"Hush, honey," Larry said. "You're making a mountain out of a molehill."

"No, Larry. That's what you did when you told me how strongly you felt."

"A long time ago—"

"Five months!"

"Can't we let this go?" He stood stalk-thin in his underwear, looking at her with annoyance.

"Yes—if you want me to believe nothing you say matters."

Quietly, he said, "That's not the point, Heidi. The point is, I owe Harold."

Heidi sat up. "Just tell me what you mean. Tell me in simple words."

"You know what I mean," Larry said, going to his backpack.

"No one gives permission for me," Heidi said. "No one."

LATER, WHILE THE OTHERS were eating dinner, Heidi packed her suitcase and let herself out of the house. The keys were still in the Jeep's ignition, and she started the motor and drove down the sandy road, bumping and splashing through puddles.

Back in her little house, she dropped her suitcase and began to turn on all the lights: the sixty-watt bulb in her mother's painted china lamp, the harsh fluorescent strips in the kitchen, the tarnished globe of the bridge lamp jettisoned from the old house. When all the lights were on, the small rooms looked pitilessly bare. The rain drummed on the flat tin roof and pinged in the bucket she'd set under a leak.

She opened the refrigerator, wanting to be hungry, wanting to cook something small and special for herself.

Her eyes fell on the plastic container where Larry had stored the casserole he'd made two nights before. She stared for a long time at the neat way the top of the container fit the bottom; she could see Larry's long fingers sealing the edges. "For Sunday," he'd said, "after we get home from your brother's."

Heidi began to cry. They were simple tears, like the rain on the flat roof that pinged from time to time in the bucket.

She was sitting at the kitchen table when Larry knocked on the door. He knocked, and waited, and knocked again, although she knew he could see her through the glass.

Finally he opened the door. "Your brother drove me back."

Heidi did not answer.

"May I come in?"

Heidi stared at the wall.

Larry stepped inside, closing the door behind him. He shrugged off his backpack and let it fall to the floor.

"Heidi," he said, "I'm sorry."

"You don't understand," she told him, and for the first time it was not a complaint or a demand but a simple statement of fact. She took some comfort from that.

Loving

Harry and I are reading the last chapter of *Ulysses*–the one we bought the book for, years ago, in Paris; we are in the middle of Molly Bloom's yeses when Harry starts to tell me about the sea cave and the girl.

Now, remember: Harry Mommoth and I have been married for twenty-seven-and-a-half years, all anniversaries and birthdays well-attended to; we have two daughters, aged twenty-five and twenty-three, and two little granddaughters–women run in my family, a fact with which Harry has easily made his peace. He believes, I think, that we are all goddesses, or at least goddesses-in-waiting, fertile with yeses, some held back willfully–just like Molly Bloom under the rhododendrons.

Harry launched into his story without preamble. "I found the sea cave, on Crete. Then I went and hung around the youth hostel in Athens until I saw a girl I wanted, and I took her back there," he tells me.

"How old were you?" I instantly want to know. Harry, at sixty-seven (we married late) has a face nearly destroyed by years in the sun—he sails, skis, only began using sunblock five years ago, under threat from his doctor—and even when I first knew him, his flimsy, flying hair was white. So I have spent half my life assembling Harry as he was, even though the few snapshots he's kept show nothing more than a shaggy boy.

"Twenty," he says. "It was the year I dropped out of Northwestern and bummed around Europe. I got lonely after six or seven months and decided to bed down on Crete. I planned to stay at least a month in the sea cave, with my pack and my sleeping bag. Nobody minded as far as I could tell."

"What was her name?"

He pretends not to remember, one of his kindly subterfuges. "Aurelia, Athena"—he has a liking for the *A*'s, perhaps because my name, Stella, is toward the other end of the alphabet.

"Oh, come on," I urge him past modesty.

"Sylvia," he admits. "From Cincinnati. She went back there, at the end of the month."

"The two of you stayed in the sea cave all that time?"

Harry doesn't answer at once. Sunday sunlight plays on the rim of my rosy teacup; *Ulysses* lies splayed on my knee. Under its weight my blue silk dressing gown—another of Harry's happy choices—is pressed out flat, and I can see the tip of my knee. We have been in bed all morning, and I am naked under the fluid silk.

"All that time," he says finally, daring to allow a little complacency into his voice.

"What did you do?"

"Fucked," he says, and now his satisfaction emerged, whole and glistening, like the freshly encapsulated bud of a purple iris.

I love his tales. I always want more.

"You had to eat now and then," I say, aiming for practicality, which cuts across my appetite in the expected way.

"There was a little trattoria—"

"Wrong country."

"Well, whatever. A little eatery on the cliff. We climbed up the path every evening at sunset, gorged ourselves on seafood, got drunk on ouzo, and tottered back down again."

"Not the best recipe for lovemaking."

"We were young. And I'm not sure I'd call it lovemaking."

I am still hungry for more details, but at the same time, he has given me enough. Harry fuels me in this way with his past, its array of astonishing images, as he fuels our little home industry—we make wooden toys—with his delightful designs, all variations on past themes: the woodchopper on Harry's wind-mill wears a pigtail and beret, the puzzle princess is a brunette, although she still sleeps on seven mattresses, each of them an oblong piece, and under them all the round wooden pea.

"I think I'll rob you of that story," I say, and before I can get too excited by the thought, I go back to *Ulysses* and finish reading the chapter.

After that we are quiet for a while. Joyce's words flit around the room like trapped sparrows. There is suddenly not enough air—winter is dissolving into spring—and I get up with a groan (the chair near the fire is so comfortable) and open a window. Beyond our porch, the Jemez Mountains are still blazing with snow, but I know it is melting, running down the arroyos to the Rio Grande.

Harry wanders over and embraces me from behind. "What are you planning to do with my story?"

"Act it," I say as his arms tighten.

"That's a great idea."

In all our years together, only my timidity has held me back. For a while I wanted him to protest more, to try to hold me, but since I was cleaving to him from the beginning like a barnacle to a rock, his wanting or not wanting to hold me came to seem immaterial. I've been to Kenya, alone, and to India with a friend, and in both places I was following Harry's footsteps, although I tried to deny it.

"It is a good idea," I say, puffing up my courage. "I've never been to Crete. It's supposed to be full of wildflowers in the spring. I'll call Donna at Whirlwind Travel tomorrow, see what the airfare costs."

"The girls are coming next Sunday," he says neutrally, knowing there's no chance I've forgotten.

I do not feel the pang or pull I expect, perhaps because he is still holding me firmly in his arms. "We'll have to put them off."

Again, his voice is neutral. "Susan and Sam started planning their trip to Italy last Christmas. They're depending on us to take the girls."

"I can't remember Christmas. Did it snow?"

"Stella, snow or no snow, you remember what you said." He does a not-entirely-kind imitation of my solicitous voice: "But we'd love to have the girls! It will be a treat for us! We never see them enough! Etcetera," he adds, unnecessarily.

"I meant it, then." I turn to face him, admiring, as I nearly always do, the glisten of his blue eyes in that flaming face. "But I've changed my mind, now. We'll just have to tell them."

He smiles, knowing I am as aware as he is of the utter unreality of such a plan. "They'll only be here two weeks."

I have nothing to say to that. After the girls' visit, there will be some other impediment. But it is not in me to remind him that we made our lives to accommodate other people: first, our daughters—and they were demanding enough, in their time; then my father, who wished, as he said, to die with us (he ended, instead, in an elegant old-age home, but that was after two years in our guest room); now our granddaughters, as well as the financial and emotional needs of friends, who pass through our house and our lives, leaving those trampling, confusing footprints you see on old, muddy trails.

"I'm afraid we're stuck," Harry says, and I realize for the first time that he never has looked forward to the little girls' visit.

I decide to take a walk and think this over. I close the Joyce and put it on the shelf we reserve for first editions, then go up to put on my jeans. There are breakfast dishes to be washed and our tumbled bed to make, but I force myself to avoid them.

Outside, the rich smell of thawing earth buoys me up, and I remember myself as a tiny child, running along a sidewalk in Cleveland with a cherry lollypop stuck in my jaw.

Spring is always late here in the Rockies; the apricots are often pinched by an April frost, but I know I will be down in my garden before long, grubbing, my hands deep in the dirt.

I'll miss the first ground-breaking, though, and I won't be able to plant vegetable seeds as I usually do indoors under the grow-light Harry fixed for me, because I'll be in Crete living in Harry's sea cave.

I have rarely done anything that surprised anyone. My fierceness, such as it is, has always been attached to appropriate tasks: I fought to have my babies without anesthetic, then breast-fed them for a full year although my mother said breast-feeding was for peasants; I found progressive yet disciplined schools for them, and labored to be an effective parent and teacher, myself. My part-time jobs while the girls were growing up were all in and around schools and libraries. Now, in retirement, Harry and I have developed his woodcarving hobby into a profitable business. The little girls have a whole collection of our toys, although I suspect they prefer plastic. So my fierceness, such as it is, has always been used appropriately, to protect and enhance this delightful life.

And now I am going to Crete, to the sea cave.

I collect a handful of pinecones, newly emerged from the snow, to dry and use for our Sunday evening fire. We'll have a good cheese omelet, a salad, a half-bottle of white wine; we are careful about our diets, about indulgences generally, although I sometimes think our marriage is the greatest indulgence of all. At night we still sleep spoon-fashion, as we did during the early, hot years. Harry's skin against mine, his hand on my belly, his faint, white smell, are the only antidotes to my sleeplessness. Away from him, I hardly close my eyes.

I know what I am going to say when I get to the kitchen door. Inside, Harry is washing the breakfast dishes. "I'd like you to consider taking care of the girls so I can go."

He looks up, not startled, but plausible, smiling. "I'm not real eager to do that."

"It's your chance." I sit down at the table, refold our napkins, elaborate. "You know when I'm around they always go to me. But they need you, Harry, and I think you need them, and with me out of the way, you'll be able to establish real relationships."

"With a three-year-old and a five-year-old?" For the first time, I detect a thread of anxiety in his voice. "You know I never had much in common with our girls until they reached the age of reason."

I remember his father, formidable even in old age, insisting that our daughters use a butter knife, not a table knife, to load their toast.

"This is your chance to change that pattern." I hardly know what I am saying, folding and refolding the soft, flowered napkins.

"I'm having a little trouble believing you mean this," Harry says.

"You've inspired me again, you should take part of the blame."

"Before, it was trips planned in advance, or learning to play the piano, or buying that scarlet dress."

"A lot of other things, too," I insist, although I am not up to making a list. "And your sea cave, unfortunately, is irresistible."

"Everything's changed. Crete certainly has. Probably there's a gate across the cave, and a guard, and a charge for going in."

"Then I'll find another. There must be a lot of them."

"You are nuts, you know that?" he says, coming over and taking hold of my hands. "I love you, and you are entirely nuts." And I realize that, finally, I have surprised him.

I go to the telephone. Talking to my oldest daughter, I detect artificiality in my voice. I sound like one of those handbooks that preach consciousness. I didn't know I was privy to this vocabulary.

To my surprise, Susan begins speaking the same tongue, and I remember that for her generation, what we would once have called pure selfishness has a variety of names. "I think it's great," she says, "if you're sure Dad is up to taking care of the girls."

"He doesn't think he is, but of course he is," I babble, staring at the Audubon wild goose hanging on the wall. The glint in the eye of the goose seems, suddenly, malevolent. "Remember when I was sick that time? He took care of you and Louise, both, very competently."

"He had Annie doing everything practical," she reminds me.

"I'll have Mercedes here, I don't expect your father to change diapers."

"Clare has been toilet-trained for the past nine months," she says severely.

"Both girls know Mercedes from your visits. They love

her!" I exclaim, perhaps a little too enthusiastically. "You and the husband-man can go to Rome and have a ball."

We share this joke title, since we both had the luck to marry uxorious men.

"Sounds like a great adventure, Mom," she says, signing off, and I remember that for her, too, the trip will be a first. "Just stay around long enough to get the girls settled, okay?"

That takes some time, several days, in fact; Clare, the younger girl, misses her mother and insists on sleeping with Harry and me, which we don't like but don't have the courage to resist. I begin to wonder whether she will sleep with Harry while I'm gone, and to imagine how she will be clinging to him by the time I come back; she is hardly old enough to hold me in her memory for two weeks. And the older girl is morose, staring out windows, asking about everything, even the cooking of hamburgers: "How long?"

But now Harry has the bit in his teeth—it seems he wants to claim these girls—and Donna at Whirlwind has found a relatively cheap fare for me. I am carried along on other people's determination that I will "have my dream," as Donna says, as though she knows me a good deal better than she does.

"Do you plan on being alone in the cave?" Harry asks the evening before I am to leave. He has drawn me a map that shows its location, on the south coast of the island.

"I don't favor hanging around youth hostels," I say, but I hear the equivocation in my voice.

"Take care of yourself, Stella," he says with a gentleness that brings tears to my eyes.

I detail all the steps I've taken to ensure that: my cell phone with its international capability, the typhoid shot my doctor didn't think I'd need until he heard where I planned to stay, the sturdy new backpack and top-quality lightweight sleeping bag I've bought. I even have new hiking boots, stout, with thickly-ridged soles. None of this, of course, means anything, but my display of all these wares allows us to end the evening peacefully.

Next morning, I'm off to the airport early, in the dark, before Harry wakes up.

On the flight to New York, I bury myself in the novel I've been trying to finish for months; alone, I don't read much, and with Harry I want to read everything out loud, which slows things down. So the four-hour flight is a luxury and a reprieve until we hit a storm west of the city and the plane begins to pitch.

I can't read anymore, and staring out the window at the armored clouds seems a mistake; the attendants have strapped themselves down, and the pilots are ominously silent. I want a word, a smile—and I turn to my seatmate, whom I have studiously avoided, and ask him to talk to me. He's a composed-

looking Japanese gentleman, and his hand looks as light as a leaf;
chatting, he lays it on mine, and the contact is reassuring. When
we land safely I thank him, and then we go our separate ways.

I have a hotel room booked for the night on the upper
East side, to be nearer to Kennedy in the morning. The hotel
has the look of a European second-class hostelry, dignified and
austere; I'm given a tiny, white bedroom facing a fire escape,
and a bathroom dark and narrow as a shoe box.

Immediately I want to go out and walk the streets, which
I do for an hour, astonished by the lushness of the goods on
display in shop windows. But everything is closed, and it is late
and wet; my hair, under my rain hat, has curled up tightly.
Finally I go back to the tiny white bedroom and try without
much success to sleep. I resist calling Harry because I know it
will mean, eventually, saying good-bye.

In the morning I'm up early—my flight to Athens doesn't
leave until late afternoon—and since my hotel has no restaurant, I hit the street. The rain has passed off during the
night, leaving the gutters running with water; people are out,
under umbrellas and raincoats, hurrying somewhere. I relish
the luxury of having the whole day to myself, of being able to
dawdle along the wet sidewalk. After a while I go into a little
coffeehouse, its window fogged by human breath.

A black woman is standing behind the high counter as
though she is at the prow of a ship. She is grand, tall, solemn,

her face shining in the dim light. Behind her the instruments of her trade are arrayed: bright, metallic espresso machines, silvery pitchers, dark square bags of coffee.

"Good morning," she says as I slide out of my raincoat. And she smiles.

It is her smile that tells me the truth of the situation: she is in charge here, she is someone to whom I owe obeisance.

"I don't know what to order," I tell her humbly because although I have been in many New York coffeehouses, this one has, suddenly, become a shrine.

"As damp and chilly as it is, I'd suggest a mocha," she says, going to work with her instruments. Her back is broad, powerful; even the skimpy, yellow uniform can't diminish it.

"I've never had a mocha," I tell her. She is surprised by this, asks where I come from, exclaims over the distance, listens with mild distraction to my commentary on my upcoming trip. When I tell her I plan to stay in a sea cave, she laughs, throwing back her head. "Where you get that idea?"

"My husband, years ago. He took a girl there."

She slides a sharp glance at me. "You going alone?"

"Yes," I say, and now I know I mean it.

Other people are coming in, ordering, settling themselves at small tables; I sit down at a shelf under the fogged window, sip my delicious mocha, and watch a bald man at the nearest table reading *The New York Times*. He is reading with great concentration, as though he is alone. I realize that I never read with that kind of concentration because I am occupied, entirely, by love.

I go back for another mocha and am a little disappointed when the black woman seems hardly to remember me; she is very busy now, I am a particle in her morning; she has assumed a larger shape in mine.

I think, suddenly, of calling Harry, and feel for my cell phone. It will still be early in the West, they will be asleep—the rosy baby girl probably tangled in Harry's arms. I put the phone away.

Later I go back to the hotel and sit in the small white bedroom, hardly denting the tightly-made bed. My gear is stacked in the corner—lumbering backpack, battered suitcase, conscientious-looking leather purse with everything that matters inside. I check my tickets and my passport for the fiftieth time, and notice that my face in the passport photo looks young and wan. I can't remember when the photo was taken— for what jaunt, real or imaginary? I go to the heavy-browed mirror to see how I look now, and my alert and sensitive, pale-blond face peers back at me as through mist.

Why am I in this hotel room? Where is it I think I'm going?

I take out my Greek guidebook, check for Harry's map, taped inside the cover, reread my itinerary, already soft from frequent foldings. I finger my traveler's checks, count the oddly-colored Greek bills Donna secured for me, pass my eyes over the little phrase book I've been studying for several days. All my tools are in place, as the black woman in the coffeehouse has hers, carefully lined up, ready to be put into service. And yet my question isn't answered.

I sit on the bed for a long time. Sunlight slices through the window, separating the iron bars of the fire escape, and I remember the wooden hotels of my childhood, near Massachusetts beaches, with fire escapes scaling down their backs. Once, I climbed down a fire escape to meet a boy I was in love with; he caught me when I dropped the final eight feet to the ground, and we stood there, pressed together, unable to separate in the soft, sea-smelling night. It has always been like that for me: I have been deeply loved, I have loved deeply, and the service of love has prepared me for what has seemed unwelcome in my life.

Harry, too, I realize, was prepared in the sea cave, all those years ago, as I have been prepared, once more, in the little coffeehouse, when the black woman smiled at me when I was drinking my first mocha, when I watched the bald man reading *The New York Times*—where nothing happened, and everything.

And so in the end I went home, not defeated, although Harry was alarmed, thinking I'd compromised.

Now, I am ready; and in the evening after the children are finally in bed, before their nightmares begin, and the distraction of consolation, I glance at Harry and see, crossing his reddened face, waves of reflected light from the blue Aegean, and I know that the same wave-light is crossing my face, scored by deepening lines, and that the light is then released into the infinite.

The Splinter

The splinter in the old woman's foot was small, a tiny darkness buried in the thick of her sole, built up by years of walking; not only walking, but skipping, hopping, jumping, and dancing well into her eightieth year. Not one of her friends was still moving, the men nearly all dead, the women humped or crushed by grief and bitterness and various (as she believed) avoidable physical ailments. Grief was not avoidable; the old woman carried hers in stone wreaths around her head and shoulders, which did not prevent her from holding her head up and her shoulders down on the dance floor, or from prancing out to perform a slow, shocking rumba.

What other people said and thought when they saw her

dancing was not what might have been expected; they stared, they clapped, and sometimes the women said incomprehensible things about joy, about gratitude, which the old woman refused to accept literally, knowing that whatever they saw had blown through her like the wind.

But she was no cave of the winds, no sibyl on her tripod, but an old woman with a birth date in the second decade of the century just passed, who had friends, and a house that needed upkeep (she climbed a ladder every fall to clear pine needles out of the gutters), and far-flung children and grandchildren whose snapshots she did not carry in her purse. In fact she did not carry a purse at all but a knapsack made out of fine soft pale leather or (for evenings) satin brocade; it was at first only this knapsack that made the young man think of her as a sort of elderly female Johnny Appleseed with all kinds of mysterious gifts and unwarranted new beginnings at her disposal.

He did not know, then, about the splinter.

They met because they shared a fence, a sagging barbed-wire fence that once in that far western place had kept sheep from wandering. When they first encountered each other over that fence (the old woman, smiling, had quoted something about good fences making good neighbors), she had shown him bunches of dingy wool from the sheep, caught long ago on the wire barbs. He'd thought, even then, when she was dressed as a country woman, with her hard-worked hands on her hips and her feet planted solidly in work boots, that she had something magical in her possession, seeds or ideas or bits of poetry, he didn't know. He agreed then and there to help her fix the wire fence, each one working from his or her side.

They arranged to do the work on a fine warm Saturday in June when the big storm clouds were just beginning to mass over the highest peak of the mountains and the soft winds of early morning were still about, bending the tips of the aspens that had barely greened up, and the pine-needle drift under their feet had the crunch of cold weather still in it. The mountain air still had a tang of the snowy winter just passed, although it was warm, and she spotted a hummingbird.

"That one belongs to me," she said as she slipped on her worn canvas work gloves, finger by finger.

"I didn't know hummingbirds belonged to anybody," the young man said, and then he watched the little thing buzzing closely around the old woman's head until she put up her hand, calmly, to fend it off, as you would fend off a molesting wasp.

"She comes and goes," the old woman said as she bent to pick up her pliers and her stout stick. The young man did not see any age in her bending and was surprised and a little discomfited because he came from a family where women over sixty generally spent a lot of time sitting down, and then had some difficulty rising from their chairs.

They both reached for the sagging top wire and he held it

taut while she grasped it with her pliers and bent it around her stick, bent it once, without much effort, and then with a groan and a strain of her freckled, pale arms, bent it again; and the wire sang as though it was a violin string. "Clamp it here," she said, and he nailed the twist into the thin old fence post and she drew her stick out of the wire circle and he nailed that, too, for good measure; and now they stood back and saw the top fence wire pulled taut and the two wires beneath it still sagging.

The old woman grasped the next wire, the middle one, with her pliers and then twisted it around her stout stick with a groan and strain and the young man nailed the twist and so they proceeded.

By noon they were both hot and tired, and he saw that her bright dyed hair was twisting into small round curls on her forehead, and then saw suddenly and without volition the baby girl of eighty-odd years before, her blond curls wet from the birth canal; and wondered. What had her life been up until that day and what had given her passion and strength, which went—but only a fraction of it, he knew already—into her twisting and straining?

"Did you grow up here?" he asked as they stood, wiping their foreheads, in a patch of shade.

"Dear me, no," she said, sounding for the first time like his grandmother sitting in her lounger in front of the TV. "I never saw the West until I was already old enough to be your mother," and he was surprised that she measured herself, even for a moment, in terms of her age relative to his.

"Where did you learn about fences?" he asked.

"Come on up to the house, I'll give you some iced tea," she said, turning to lead him off through the piñons, "and then I'll tell you," and the young man followed as young men sometimes follow witches or the fairy godmothers of their beloveds in the old stories.

The old woman lived not in a gingerbread cottage but in a fine new house set on a crest among the pines. The kitchen she led him into was bright, scoured, glasses and dishes flashing on open shelves, silvery faucets and knobs each reflecting tiny rainbows of sun. The table she sat him down at was a clean pine board and the glass of pale-brown tea she put in front of him was decorated with a sprig of mint and a slice of lemon; and there was a china plate, with roses around the rim, stacked with small lemon cookies, which she put on the table between them before taking her place.

"I don't know anything about fences," she told him, sitting down, and he knew her stout boots were aligned opposite his sneakers under the table, toes to toes. "I make it up as I go along. There's probably a right way to tighten wire fences, a way they teach you in ag school or you could read up on in books, but I have my own way which works pretty well." She pushed the china plate toward him and he took one of the tiny lemon cookies and let it melt on his tongue before he asked, "Do you make up everything as you go along?"

"Pretty much," she said. "I lost everything and everybody early in life and after that it seemed the only way to go on was to make things up, because the guides and the counselors were gone, all dead early from various sicknesses and wars. I don't regret any of it," she said. "I never would have learned if I hadn't been on my own from so early."

"I've had family every inch of the way," he said, thinking of the way they still clustered around him—and he was in his mid-twenties, grown, after all—with marriages and baptisms and funerals and all the meals that went with those occasions, and the phone calls and cards. His family was around him like the soft feathers that line a wren's nest, and like feathers they some-times got into his nose and clogged his breathing or caused a fit of sneezing; but he was grateful for the softness they pro-vided as he made his way in the world. Other than family, he had nothing to call his own but the bit of land that abutted the old woman's land, which he had inherited from an uncle, the old sheepherder whose flock had once grazed there.

"Were you married?" he asked, because it seemed the only way to open up her history. All the women he knew, all the older women, at least, were married or had been married and made long, engrossing, and sometimes funny stories out of that. His aunt, the first person divorced in his family, entertained at Thanksgiving with stories of her ex-husband's misdeeds, still fresh, though he'd been gone for more than twenty years, and his grandmother who seemed as ancient as mountain rock crowed now and then about a romance in her far-off youth, somewhere in Mexico.

"Oh yes," she said. "We all were, in those days. It didn't amount to much, to tell you the truth. I loved him for a while, and he loved me, and then that ended, and we didn't know how to go on. I thought I was dying of starvation but of course I was just hungry from immaturity—all the experiences I hadn't tasted and wasn't likely to taste in a nice house outside of Baltimore. There would have been children and I didn't want children, then." She took a sip of her tea and wiped her mouth on the back of her hand, and he noticed that her lips were soft and rosy inside their net of radiating lines, so that her mouth, he thought, suddenly (and again, this was unwilled) was like a rosy little insect, a spider, even, set inside its fine net.

He thought she was finished and wanted to find a way to get her to go on when she went on of her own accord. "The second one I was madly in love with and it lasted longer and there was a child and I adored the child, my only son, but then time happened as it always does and everything fell apart. It seemed I fell apart because I was in love with another man but really it was just the passage of time."

"So the other man—?"

"He was married, there was nothing to do about it. His wife asked me very nicely to leave him alone and of course I did. I've never been able to resist nice women asking me to do something that obviously I should be doing without being asked." She laughed and reached for a cookie, which she ate with two bites, not allowing it time to melt on her tongue, as the young man had, out of politeness and appreciation.

Now the sun of early afternoon was coming through the window, patching bright squares on the pine table, and her hands in that scalding light were spotted like two small animals that carry the marks of their breed. He wondered at her pink fingernails which were somehow preserved in spite of her hard work–for he knew, now, without being told, that she did all the work on her few acres–and also wondered about the small winking diamond she wore on her ring finger.

"The third one was sexy as hell, I enjoyed him a lot, and I was getting older by then and needed him for reassurance," she said, moving her hands out of the light, and he wondered for the first time if she was vain. In the shadow her hands looked pale and genteel, and he wanted to tell her that he preferred the small spotted animals. "But he ran off with another woman and that was the end of that, as it always is," she said, and he wondered why there was no dying fall to her voice as there was when his aunt and his grandmother came to the end of their tales. "And then I came out West."

"And since then—?"

"Alone, thank God." She saw him glance at her ring. "When the last one left, I bought myself this; it cost a pretty penny," she said. "I won't take it off, they'll have to bury it with me—it's grown into my finger." She demonstrated by trying to pull it off; the ring was incised in a groove he imagined deepening every time she turned over in her sleep. And for the first time since he'd met her, he wished something.

She went on, "I have my old-man friends who take me out to dinner now and then but none of them has the energy to do more. Oh, they'd respond if I started something, and maybe for a few hours or even a few days it would seem like the old times, hot and vivid, but none of them could keep it up and to tell the truth, I probably couldn't either. Besides, I love living alone." She stood up to take the iced-tea glasses to the sink. "You live with someone?" she asked.

He wanted to say, "Of course," but instead he said only, "Yes."

"Good-looking, I bet," the old woman said, turning to face him.

Ordinarily the young man would have answered, "Certainly," and have been even a little insulted that anyone could imagine he would live with someone who was not good-looking. But now the automatic answer slid from his lips and he found himself pondering. Who was he, really, the man who had shared his bed and his life for five years?

"His name's Elton," he said, aware that the old woman was not surprised. "He's forty years old. We've lived together for more than five years."

"My Lord," the old woman said, still facing him from the sink, "he got you early."

Again his ability to be offended seemed to shrink and he found himself smiling as he answered, "Just out of college."

"Oh, how do they do it," she murmured, but it was not a question. It was a statement of admiration, of kinship, even. "With some magical combination of charm and stability, the way in the old days older men wooed younger women. I always thought it was the promise of monogrammed sheets and family china."

He was still smiling when he said, "Well, maybe something like that. Elton doesn't support me, though," and wondered why it suddenly didn't matter, that statement he'd made so often to friends and acquaintances and even strangers, as though his pride or even his sense of himself depended on it. "He did buy our house but my name's on the deed," and the satisfaction he usually felt when he said that was smaller, too.

"That's what my first husband did, and I liked it so much," she said. "I thought it meant I was home forever."

"This is going to last," the young man said with the conviction that had grown firm over five years of pot roasts and Sunday visits to his family and vacations in Hawaii. "We even know where we're going to be buried," and he wanted to take the old woman to see the little graveyard back in the mountains, gay as a dance hall with plastic flowers.

"Together?" she asked, as though only that would surprise her.

He nodded. "We've made all the arrangements, even decided what we want on the stone."

"What?" she asked.

"'Together in life,'" he said, "'Together in death'"—and suddenly it seemed faintly, but only faintly, ridiculous. Perhaps they should search for a line of poetry.

"That's on my parents' grave," she said. "They're buried together, too, or at least their coffins are side by side. I don't think two people can really be buried together."

"Well, close, anyway," he said, and thought of the big bed where he and Elton ended up, most mornings, wedged into a corner, sheets and blanket spreading out like an unnecessary ocean.

"I imagine we are the only two people on this mountain talking about our graves," she said, leading the way to the door and pulling on her gloves.

"You haven't told me about yours," he said, hurrying along behind. She was nimble, she was fast, and he wondered how long it would be before she wore out.

"Well, I've chosen the spot, but I haven't gotten around to choosing the epitaph," she told him over her shoulder. "Come on, I'll show you," and she led him to a little grove of scraggly piñons on a rock crest. The valleys spread out below them blue and hazy, as it was always blue and hazy now, with the Western range rearing up thirty miles away. "Right here," she said, stamping her foot, "among rocks and trees."

"They may have trouble digging," he said.

"They can bring in a backhoe." She turned to lead him away to the fence. "A friend of mine's going to make me a pine box and fill it with leaves."

All that afternoon as it grew hotter and dustier they worked on tightening the fence, and the young man waited for the old woman to wear out. It was not that he enjoyed the prospect of seeing her exhausted but that he wanted to be of greater help than he was when he merely nailed her twists to the fence posts. She still groaned on the second twist and now her pale, freckled arms were damp with sweat, but she did not seem to be exerting any more effort than she had in the morning.

By four o'clock, the young man realized she was probably not going to wear out, realized it with a keenness of disappointment that surprised him, although he had already imagined bringing her water or offering his bandanna so she could wipe her forehead, had already imagined giving her his arm as she staggered toward the house. It was not so much the physical contact he'd wished for, although he found he was not repelled by that, but the belief that he existed in her life, that he had a role to play beyond that of an attentive young man holding a hammer and nails. But she did not fail, and when the last strand was tightened, she simply turned away and started toward the house.

It was a minute before he noticed she was limping.

He hurried behind her. "Are you hurt?"

She turned, and for the first time he saw something like bleakness in her face. "Just a splinter," she said. "I was garden-ing barefoot yesterday and I think I must have stepped on a pinecone, you know they have those sharp little spurs."

Now he did offer her his arm, with a gesture he realized he had never in his life made before, a gesture solemn and silly as a courtier's in a ritual procession. He did not think she was a queen or a saint, but when she put her spotted hand in the crook of his arm and he felt her fingers against his skin, he knew there was something in the touch of her warm, damp fingers that he had never imagined before. He was ordinarily rather squeamish, repelled by wetness and odors, and the wetness and the odors emitted by women were a blackness in his life and had been since he was a small child. But this contact with the old woman's five fingers was what he could only call "clean," although "clean" was without power and would not do. So she leaned on him as they went up the path, and he continued to feel her warm, moist skin.

His mother had said to him once—and it was the only time she'd broached the subject—that aversion was not a sound basis for a relationship. The words had not been those, of course; she had hinted and stalled, but he had known what she meant and had flushed hot with rage. As though his faithful and persistent love, for which he was grateful every day of his life, could be reduced to that—a cowardly fleeing. He had not forgiven his mother, yet.

The remembered comment stung him now as it had the first time and he suddenly withdrew his arm.

She did not seem to notice, going along ahead of him, slowly, now, with her limp.

"Which foot is it?" he asked.

"Left," she said, softly, as though this, at last, was a secret. "I tried to get the splinter out but I couldn't do it."

He realized this was what he had been waiting all day to hear.

He hurried after her. "I took a splinter out of Elton's foot, a really bad one, last week," he said. "We thought he'd have to see a doctor, but I did it"—and he remembered his lover's groan as he pried at the splinter in his heel with a needle.

"Then maybe you should try," she said, in an ordinary way, as though they were talking about some meaningless errand. And she went into her kitchen.

The sun was in the west now, and the kitchen was full of silky shadows. Even the pine table that had gleamed earlier with reflected light was dark as a negative from which the colored print had been taken.

She sat down on the bench beside the table and began to unlace her boot, and he noticed how slowly her little spotted hands moved now.

"I'll get you a glass of water," he said.

She did not reply and he went to the sink and ran a glass full of cool water and brought it to her. "Do you want ice?"

"No," she said, so faintly now, so far away he wondered if she was even aware of his hovering presence. "Ice hurts my teeth."

He sat down on the other end of the bench and waited while she peeled off her damp socks, and again he was aware of not being revolted, of not wanting to turn his head away. He reached for her socks in a matter-of-fact way and rolled them together, feeling her sweat on his fingers. He laid the rolled-up socks on the bench between them and looked down at her long, white feet on the pine floor. She was wearing scarlet nail polish.

Then he took her left foot in his hand. Her toughened heel

lay in his right palm and his left hand closed over her instep and he sat for a moment without moving or speaking.

"I have big feet," she said.

He did not reply. In his right palm her heel weighed solidly and he could feel the arch of her instep with his left. It was like, he thought, the arch of a strong doorway, reaching up, while the weight of the stones sank toward the ground. He had never thought such a thing before and yet it did not surprise him, as though the perception had simply waited, like a seed, for a drop of moisture to cause it to sprout.

"The tweezers are right here where I left them when I had to give up," she said, reaching for a little basket of odds and ends that sat on the ledge above the table. She took out a pair of tweezers and handed them to him. "Don't hurt me," she said.

He did not reply because he knew she knew there was no such assurance to be made. Instead he turned her foot so that the sole faced toward him and looked for the splinter, feeling with his forefinger.

"Ouch," she said, as his finger pressed into a dark dot beneath her big toe.

He peered and saw the splinter. It was rather deeply buried in the calluses there.

"I'll have to dig a little," he said. "Do you have a needle, and matches?"

She gestured toward the little basket, and he found a red pincushion shining with needles and a book of matches. As he took these things out, he saw that the matches were from the restaurant where he and Elton had gone to celebrate their last anniversary.

He transferred her foot to his knee and chose a long, sharp needle and lit a match and carefully burned the needle's tip in the flame. He wanted to say something about always being careful but it seemed unnecessary.

"Are you always careful?" she asked.

"Yes," he said, hearing the resonance. "I am always careful. I grew up knowing I would always have to be careful."

"I'm glad," she said.

"Elton grew up thinking the world was wide open, everything was possible—and safe," he said, bending with his needle over her sole. "He's angry, now that everything is dangerous."

"Are you going to hurt me?" she asked.

"Maybe," he said, and he shook the needle tip to cool it. Then he studied the splinter under her skin. "You've walked it right up into your foot, you should have done something about it before. Elton's was the same way, he walked on it for four days before he decided to let me get it out." He remembered Elton slipping off his loafer while he stood over him with the sterilized needle. "I needed a magnifying glass for his, I don't need it for yours," he added, as though the difference had some significance.

And he pushed the needle in.

She cried out.

He tightened his hold on her foot so she couldn't jerk it away and said, "I have to get under the splinter to get it out," firmly, as though he was speaking to a frightened child.

"Oh, please," she said, laying her hand on his arm, but he shrugged her hand off and pried with the needle again. A drop of blood rose to the surface and ran down her heel.

"I'm going to get it out," he said, and with one more push, one more cry, he'd laid the dark end of the splinter bare.

Still holding her foot firmly, he reached with his free hand for the tweezers and, frowning to see more clearly, grasped, after two tries, the end of the splinter, and pulled it free. A few drops of blood followed.

"You hurt me!" she wailed, and when he looked at her, he saw she had tears in her eyes.

"All better now," he said gruffly, because his heart was moved. "Do you have any antiseptic?"

"In the closet," she said.

He knew it was safe, now, to let her foot go—she would not try to escape—and so he went to the closet and found hydrogen peroxide and cotton. When he came back she was keening, like a woman at some old-fashioned funeral, and he stood for a moment behind her, looking down at her bright, damp hair. "You know I had to do it," he said.

"I even asked you to," she said, laughing through her tears. "The more fool me."

"Once this has healed, you won't have to limp anymore," he said as he swabbed her foot with the antiseptic. "Do you have any dry socks?"

"Yes," she said, wearily now, as though the ordeal had, finally, exhausted her, and he followed her up the stairs to her bedroom. She turned on the top step and glanced at him, and he realized that she was surprised, but he did not feel a need to explain. He stood in the bright box of a room with its view over the mountains and studied her bed, flossy with embroidered sheets and lace pillowcases. "For the princess who sleeps on a pea," he said when she turned from the bureau, holding a pair of socks.

She came then and put her arms around him, and it seemed natural and even commonplace to put his arms around her. For the first time, he realized that she was his height, so that when she laid her cheek against his, they were perfectly aligned like, he thought, two figures in an old frieze.

"You hurt me," she said thoughtfully.

"I had to," he said.

Then they drew apart as though by mutual impulse, and he followed her down the stairs. In the kitchen, she sat down on the bench and held out the socks, and he took them and separated them and drew them one at a time over her long white feet. The socks were printed with butterflies in many colors. "Pretty," he said when she arched her feet, showing him how the butterflies moved over her instep, and he remembered how that strong, naked arch had felt under his hand.

He stood up then, thinking of time and the fence done and Elton waiting at home. There were many questions he had not thought to ask, and now he knew there was no need for questions or for answers. Under the butterfly sock, the tiny hole he'd made with the needle was slowly closing, the quick healing of her sturdy old body taking care of that; but perhaps in time to come she would see as she pulled on socks or stockings a tiny, an infinitesimal, white scar, there under her big toe.

"We were just going to fix the fence," she said. "Are you leaving now?"

"Yes," he said, and knew he would always be leaving, and always coming back.

The Author

Susan Hazen-Hammond

SALLIE BINGHAM's first novel was published by Houghton Mifflin in 1961. It was followed by two collections of short stories, four novels, and a memoir. Her short stories have been published in *The Atlantic Monthly, New Letters, Plainswoman, Plainsong, The Greensboro Review, Negative Capability, The Connecticut Review,* and *Southwest Review,* among others. Her stories have been included in *Best American Short Stories, Forty Best Stories from* Mademoiselle, *Prize Stories: The O. Henry Awards,* and *The Harvard Advocate Centennial Anthology.* She has received fellowships from Yaddo, The MacDowell Colony, The Virginia Center for the Creative Arts, and The Vermont Studio Center. She was Book Editor for *The Courier-Journal* in Louisville and has been a director of the National Book Critics Circle. She is the founder of The Kentucky Foundation for Women and *The American Voice.*